Joy Cometh
in the
MORNING

SARAH ANKNEY

ISBN 978-1-63903-554-0 (paperback)
ISBN 978-1-63903-555-7 (digital)

Christian Faith Publishing
832 Park Avenue
Meadville, PA 16335
www.christianfaithpublishing.com

Printed in the United States of America

To the Lord and in memory of my parents. Mom passed away before reaching a hundred years old. In memory of my first-grade teacher and second mom, Barbara Dunham, and also in memory of my dear friend, Leora Petet.

Contents

1

The Surprise

Charles Johnson's six-foot-three-inch frame sank behind his steering wheel in disbelief. After his shift at the plant, he would happily get in the car, toss his dented lunchbox in the backseat, turn the radio on, and make the eighteen-minute drive home. But today was different.

He thought back to the sage advice his dad and grandfather had given him while growing up. Do your best and you'll never lack a job. Stay with the same company, and as you help it grow, your job security will also grow. Charles followed that advice.

He started working part-time summers for the fabrication factory. Upon high school graduation, he was hired full-time. Over the years, he worked his way up to shift supervisor. He got along with coworkers, plus he also had a talent for design. The company's owners even asked his input at times when there was a problem with a product.

He was thirty-seven years old and had worked full-time for twenty years. "So why am I holding a pink slip?" he thought out loud while turning the key in the ignition. "Lord, what did I do wrong? How in the world do I tell Kay? You know today is our fifteen wedding anniversary. How do I tell her that in two weeks, I will be out of a job? I have a high school diploma. Since I had a good job, there was no need to worry about going to college and its expense. What do I do now? I cannot let Kay and the kids down. They depend on me. What happens next? Help me. Jesus, please answer me." Silence.

Suddenly Charles was startled by the crackle of radio static. While still praying—out of habit, he had turned the radio on. A Christian station was on. The words came out loud and clear—one day at a time! Okay, Lord, show me day by day.

Just then, Charles glanced down at his watch. Months before, he had put a small diamond necklace on lay away. The last twenty-five-dollar payment was due today. He had a fleeting thought about canceling the gift and getting the money refunded. He loved Kay dearly, but with today's news, maybe the money could be used for needed bills.

Then he said, "I cannot do that to Kay. Why should my job loss spoil her happiness today? I will tell her after our anniversary." He hurried to the jewelry store before it closed.

Arriving home with the special gift wrapped package safely hidden deep in his trouser pocket, he reached for the doorknob. The front door swung open, and there stood their eldest, twelve-year-old James Robert Johnson.

"Hi, Dad," said James. Before Charles could say anything, Charles and Kay's youngest child, precious five-year-old Evelyn Grace, raced to the door.

"Daddy, what took you *so* long?" Evelyn Grace asked as she shook her finger at her dad. Mommy's got supper ready. Susie is helping her set the table. Daddy, hurry up. We're all starving."

"You mean you're starving," Charles said as he smiled at his younger daughter.

"Come back to the dining room," called Kay. "The pot roast is done."

"The pudding I made for dessert is in the fridge," said eight-year-old Susie Kay Johnson proudly.

"Okay," exclaimed Charles, "we are coming."

After dinner, the kids raced into the family room. "What's going on?" Charles inquired of Kay.

Kay shrugged her shoulders and answered, "I'm not sure what they are up to?" She smiled. "But I think we will soon find out."

"Mom, Dad, hurry up. Have we got a surprise for you." The children almost shouted with anticipation. As Charles and Kay sat on the sofa, little Evie handed Kay a package and said with glee, "Mommy, you go first."

Kay handed Charles his gift. He laughed out loud when he opened the gift, a gleaming new all-metal lunchbox and thermos. "Thank you, honey."

Kay said, "I had quite a search for it. It's about time to retire your grandfather's old lunchbox so you can keep it as a family heirloom before it falls apart."

"This new one is larger, so you'll have room for a mid-shift snack, Daddy," added Susie.

"Okay, Dad, it's your turn," quipped James Robert.

As Charles reached into his pocket, Evie exclaimed, "The box is so little. I hope you got Mommy a nice gift."

"Evelyn Grace Johnson," exclaimed her shocked siblings.

"It's such a tiny box." Evie sighed.

"What a dumb thing to say," replied James Robert and just shook his head.

Charles spoke up, "Evie Grace, you have to learn not to be so outspoken about things."

"Okey dokey, Daddy. I'll try to remember," answered Evelyn Grace.

Charles continued, "The value of a gift is not totally based on the size of the gift. What's more important is what that gift means both to the giver as well as the one receiving it." He passed the brightly wrapped package with a card that read, "To my beloved wife, Kay, the love of my life."

Kay's eyes filled with tears of joy as she said, "Oh, hon, I love you." And she gave Charles a big kiss.

"Way to go, Dad," exclaimed James Robert and Susie Kay in unison.

"Now it's our turn," said Evie Grace as she jumped up and down excitedly. She handed a large handmade card to James and Susie. They proudly handed the colorful anniversary card to their parents.

"What did you guys do?" questioned Charles.

"Read the card, Daddy," said Susie. "Happy Anniversary to the greatest parents."

"Don't forget to look inside," shouted Evie.

As Charles and Kay opened the card, a gift certificate fell out.

"To the recipient, a free ten-day stay at Peaceful Valley Bed and Breakfast."

Taped to the certificate were train tickets to their vacation and back. Charles and Kay looked at each other in total surprise.

"How did you pull this off without us knowing anything?" asked Kay.

James answered, "We have been planning this for a year. I used money from shoveling snow and mowing lawns."

"I helped rake lawns," said Susie.

"I put the raked piles in garbage bags," added little Evie Grace.

"Granddad Johnson and Granddad Kuntz helped too! It's all been set up for seven weeks from now. School will be out. Mom's job as a teacher will also be done for the summer," said Susie.

"That also gives you time to put in for vacation time at work, Dad," said James.

"No problem," said Charles quietly.

"Mommy and Daddy, don't worry about us while you're gone," added Susie.

"We'll have two vacations," piped up Evie Grace.

"She means," James Robert clarified, "we will stay half the time with Granddad and Grandma Johnson and the rest of the time with Granddad and Grandma Kuntz."

"It looks like everything is set," said Kay.

"I think you're right," answered Charles. He smiled and tried to seem excited about the kids' gift. But in the back of his mind, he was wondering about a new job. After the children were asleep, Charles checked the doors and windows. He also looked in on the children again before putting the lights out.

When he returned to the bedroom, Kay was waiting for him. Kay said, "I love the necklace, but what are you not telling me?"

"What do you mean?" asked Charles.

"Your answer to James about scheduling the time off. You were too quiet. What is wrong?"

"I did not want to ruin the day for everyone," Charles admitted. He took a deep breath and blurted out about the pink slip and pending job loss. "The owners want to retire but could not find a buyer for the company. So it's closing. I'm too young to retire. They had a meeting for all the employees. Everyone can move their pensions and will get a severance package. One week's pay for every year of service. In my case, twenty weeks. Then I will have six months unemployment. Kay, you have your job teaching so we won't have any problems for a while. But can I find a good job without a college degree?"

Kay took his hand firmly in her hand and said, "This could mean it's time for a change. Maybe it's time you followed your dream of being of being an architect."

"I've read a lot of books on architecture. So I took some online courses in architecture when James was little, but that is nowhere near a degree. I know the kids worked hard for our gift, but will I lose valuable time job hunting?"

"Charles, listen to me," implored Kay. "You are still in shock over the company's decision. We'll tighten the budget. You know I'm pretty good at finding stuff on sale." Charles gave a weak smile.

"Let's not disappoint the children. You can job search before and during the trip," Kay added.

"Take the laptop along to check your emails and research jobs. Just make sure you add your cell phone number to your résumé. This anniversary vacation the family has given us will give us a much-needed chance to rest. Not only that but we will be better prepared to make any decisions about our future."

"You're right, Kay. It's just I cannot seem to shake the feeling as a husband, father, and breadwinner I'm a failure to you and the kids."

"Charles Johnson, I will not stand for you thinking that way. You're a wonderful loving husband and father. You're a caring, compassionate Christian man. Do you understand, Charles? You are a man—you are not perfect. None of us are. You have no control over the situation. So quit blaming yourself," Kay said as she gave Charles a hug.

"We need to pray," she added as she took her husband's hand again. "Dear Lord, only you know the future. Guide us to the right job for Charles. Teach us daily to look to you as the ultimate provider—Jehovah Jireh. Show us where you want us to be and give us your peace while we wait for the answer. Thank you, Jesus, the only begotten Son of God and our Savior. We'll leave things in your capable hands. Amen." And with that, Kay looked Charles in eye. "It will be all right!" She then gave him a good-night kiss, put out the light, and rolled over in bed to sleep.

Charles lay there in the darkness a moment. Then he looked toward the ceiling and quietly whispered, "Lord, just help me with my faith and patience to wait on your perfect timing." Then he closed his eyes to rest.

2

Can This Be for Real?

With only four days left until the factory closing, Charles had just finished final shift schedules for his section of the plant when he heard someone calling him. He looked up from his paperwork to see Mr. Logan, an owner of the company.

"Hey, Charles," said David Logan, "there is another meeting in half an hour. We need you there. It's important."

"I'll be there."

I wonder what *is happening,* Charles thought as he walked into the conference room. The massive room was packed with people. In some areas of the conference room, it was standing room only. The entire Logan family was there as well. Another owner motioned for Charles to take a seat at one end of a very long table.

Then Martin Logan, a senior owner of the company, stepped to the podium. "We realize our business has been in this community for many decades. Older members of our family want to retire while the younger members have other business interests. They want to sell. I'm sure you're all aware of the rough economy. A small group of employees are trying to get a business loan and credit line for working capital. I hope they succeed.

"We will have an answer in a week. If they can get the funding, everyone's jobs will be saved. Everything will still operate the same way. That is the best scenario. If not..." Martin Logan sighed. "My family has an alternative plan. The employees as a whole form a cor-

13

poration to buy the business. The purchase price would be funded by relinquishing a large portion of your severance pay. So we will have another meeting in a week. Please come prepared to vote on plan two if the loan falls through."

Charles Johnson looked around the room at a sea of solemn faces and silence. A few minutes later, people slowly started to file out of the conference room. They were talking in hushed whispers and shaking their heads.

Charles stood up and was turning to go when David Logan said, "We still need to talk to you. Charles, my family truly wishes plan one works. But we have to be realistic. If there is a vote, it would require 75 percent of employees agreeing to plan two. If neither plan happens, the building will be sold."

"What does that have to do with me?" asked Charles.

"We need someone who understands all parts of the factory. We checked the records. Over the years, you have worked in all areas of the plant. If needed, we want you to pick a group of employees for an important project. You will be given complete control of this group to dismantle, box, and store all equipment. It will take a couple of weeks. If you do it in three weeks, each employee will earn an extra week in severance pay as a bonus. Will you do it?" asked David Logan.

Charles took a deep breath. Slowly he nodded his head and said, "Yes, but I hope things work out that the equipment won't be dismantled."

"Fair enough," exclaimed Martin Logan. "We'll see what happens a week from now."

Charles could hardly believe what he had been asked to do. He had an awful lot to discuss with Kay.

When he had arrived home, Kay said, "A coworker has a relative who works at the plant too. All she told me there was a big meeting. I made the kids supper already so we can talk privately. They are upstairs doing homework."

"That's good," said Charles with a sigh. "We have a lot to talk about. Kay, when I started working there, I would have never dreamed a meeting like this would ever happen. First, there is a possible buyer. Second, the Martin family is offering a company buyout to the employees. If neither plan works out, Kay, the Martins want me to head the equipment dismantle team. If we finish in three weeks, everyone gets another severance week bonus."

"That was some meeting," said Kay. "What do you think will happen?"

"I don't know. I wish things could continue at before. I hate the idea of starting over. We have a little savings. There is still eleven years left in our mortgage. James Robert will be going to college in about six years. The way the Logans are talking, I think they doubt that the buyers will get the necessary funding."

"Well, you mentioned there was another option?"

"Kay, how do you feel about giving up half or more of my severance with no guarantee of success?"

"I'm not sure. It's a little overwhelming to try to consider everything."

"When the Logans were dealing with customers or bidding big contracts, only a couple people were needed to approve and sign off on stuff. Would a corporation's board slow acceptance of contracts? It usually takes a couple of years for any business to be profitable. This would probably mean lower paychecks until the company became profitable again. Could we pay our bills and make due until then?"

"You are asking something I cannot answer. How many repeat customers will continue contracts? Or will it be starting from scratch?"

"Good questions. I don't know."

"If you don't think that will work and you don't want to start over in a different place, how is the local job search going?"

"It's hard because so many plant employees are also looking locally. Initially I submitted my résumé to forty local companies. I got four interviews. The outcome—one business said that I needed a college degree. Two said with my work experience, I was overqualified. And the last one said they would call me if there was an opening, but it could be up to a year of longer. I've emailed résumés to an additional twenty local companies. I even asked if anyone at church knew of anyone anywhere was hiring. The pastor said since quite a large number of members are working at the plant, the church is planning a bus trip to a job fair in Clarksburg this Saturday."

"That's sixty miles from here," exclaimed a shocked Kay. "Well, the kids are going to a birthday party Saturday. I'll be doing spring cleaning and praying too. As far as the company vote goes, I will let that up to you. Whatever you decide, I'll stand with you."

"Thanks, honey," said Charles. "I guess it's time to say hello to the kids." He headed for the stairs.

The next day, Charles stopped off at the personnel office to check employee records to begin making plans on picking the dismantle team. There were fifteen separate divisions in the plant. He chose fifty employees—a team of two from each area with an additional twenty to help as needed. He held his special meeting in the morning the day before the plant's last official day of work. A few of the people knew Charles well. The rest were just happy to know that they would have three more weeks of work if the business really did close for good. All of them were willing to be on the team.

By noon that day, Charles was required to turn in his plans for the dismantle team. He did and asked the Logans if there was an answer to the buyout business loan. There was no answer yet.

On the last day of production, the plant only operated until one in the afternoon. After that, the Logans planned a plant-wide retirement party for any employee who had already reached retirement or who would be retiring. In reality, it was actually a goodbye party for everyone. There was a plant-wide gift giveaway for everyone. Charles thought the party seemed more like a giant Christmas party except the atmosphere was bittersweet for the unknown. Each employee received a gift certificate to a grocery store.

After the party, Martin Logan read a short retirement speech and thanked all employees for their quality of work and loyalty. Martin Logan said, "I feel like I'm saying goodbye to family." He paused. "Enjoy your weekend and please pray for our last meeting on Monday afternoon at three. Also before leaving, everyone stop at loading dock 4."

Charles punched his timecard one last time and grabbed his new lunchbox filled with leftover cake and goodies. He put his last paycheck and grocery gift certificate in his pocket. When he arrived at the loading dock, he could not believe his eyes. There were several truckloads of canned goods, fruit, and cases of pop. Each employee was given boxes of canned goods, assorted fruit, and a case of pop.

With the car packed with boxes, Charles headed home. Once he pulled into the driveway, he wondered how many trips would be needed to unload the car. As Charles neared the porch, he yelled for someone to open the door.

Kay came looking surprised. "Don't tell me you robbed a grocery store," she said with a grin.

"Kay, they were so nice and then even giving food away. I just wish there was an answer about the business loan."

"Well, don't forget you have to be at the church early tomorrow. Pastor Evans called. The bus is leaving at *6:30 a.m.* They want to arrive at the job fair before the doors open."

"I did not forget, Kay, that you said you'll be spring cleaning tomorrow. The sooner you start, the sooner you will be done."

"Charles Johnson, you know I cannot spring clean a two-story house in one day."

"Oh, I thought you could," Charles said and laughed.

"Well, call the kids. We need help unloading the car. Then we better get supper and have a little family time before going to bed early."

After dinner as Charles opened his lunchbox, James Robert, Susie Kay, and Evelyn Grace looked on in surprise as Charles pulled out big slices of cake and cookies.

Evie asked, "Where did all that stuff come from?"

"There was a party at work and the bosses sent goodies home with everyone."

"We'll celebrate the last day of school," exclaimed James and Susie. "No homework tonight, so why don't we play Monopoly?"

"Okay."

Two hours later, Charles looked at the mantle clock—bedtime for everyone. Before Charles and Kay knew it, the alarm was going off at quarter till 5:00 a.m. Charles and Kay grabbed a quick breakfast, and Charles was off to the church.

17

As Charles pulled up to the church parking lot got out of the car, he could not believe how many people were there. Pastor Evans was standing in the center of the parking lot.

Pastor Evans said, "We had so many people inquiring about the job fair we needed two buses. The deacons and trustees have also provided for everyone's meals. So before you board the buses, let's have a prayer.

"Dear Lord, we praise your holy name. Please give us traveling mercies. Also lead people to the right job for each one, and we give all the praise and glory to you. In Jesus's name, we pray."

As the pastor finished, sunlight broke through gray clouds and down on the large group. The people hurried to get on the buses. The caravan headed to the job's fair with high hopes.

3

Train Ride

"We only have short time to get the car loaded, get you kids dropped off at Granddad and Grandma Kuntz, and get to the station. Kay stood in the living room with checklist in hand. Charles, James Robert, the suitcases are packed and are at the top of the stairs. Please bring them down. Susie Kay and Evelyn Grace, did you gather up the toys that you're taking? Also, James, did you get your laptop and your dad's?"

"Yes, Mom. They're already in the car," answered James.

"Son, did you charge your cell phone last night?"

"Yes."

"Charles, do you have your briefcase for job searching?"

"Yes, dear, and my phone charger is in it too. Since the vote on Logan Fabrication ended in closure of the plant, my phone is fully charged and is in my pocket. I also printed out a couple dozen résumés yesterday. They are in my briefcase. I'm all set to find a job even while we are on our anniversary trip."

Kay sounding like a drill sergeant ordered Charles and James, "Finish loading the car while I make sure the windows are closed, stove and coffee pot are off, and the doors locked."

"Honey," said Charles, "I realize you don't want to forget anything. Just relax."

As she finished, everyone piled into the car. Kay looked into the backseat of the SUV. "Listen to your grandparents. Remember, then in a week, Granddad and Grandma Kuntz will drive you to Granddad and Grandma Johnson. We'll pick you up when we get back."

"Mom, just chill," said James Robert. "We'll be fine. You and Dad just enjoy your time at Peaceful Valley Bed and Breakfast. You'll see some beautiful scenery as the train travels through miles of countryside. We got you a disposable camera to record memorable images."

"Thank you, guys," said Kay as Charles pulled out of the driveway and headed toward the end of town where Kay grew up.

The kids quickly grabbed their stuff, called goodbye, and ran inside their grandparents' home.

Kay looked sad as Charles said, "We better get going or we'll miss the train. What time is the train leaving the depot?"

Kay pulled the schedule out of her purse, "Ten a.m."

"It's nine thirty now. How long is the train ride?"

"Eighteen hours. It meanders through farmlands, forests, and rugged granite mountains and ends near a large picturesque lake with the bed and breakfast on a bluff overlooking the lake."

They arrived and found their spot on the train. To their surprise, the family had paid for a private compartment. Kay seemed overwhelmed with the apparent care and thoughtfulness to detail to give them a well-deserved vacation. She felt tears coming as she sank into the comfy, plush deep-blue overstuffed upholstery. She gazed out the window waiting for the train to leave the station. Charles held her close and wiped her tears away.

"These are tears of happiness, not sadness," said Kay.

"I know we are going through a lot. And we are dealing with an uncertain future. We will have this time to discuss and plan what to do. But let's not let our current situation keep us from enjoying what our kids and parents have given us. James Robert, Susie Kay, and Evelyn Grace have worked hard to plan and implement this vacation for us."

"You're right. We can't disappoint them," Kay replied.

"When I was at the job fair, I submitted résumés and applications to what seemed like a couple hundred companies. I gave them my cell number and email address. I had already set up an email just for new applications. That way, I'll be able to keep track of new and older job opportunities easily. I'l check things in the morning and evening. But, Kay, my beautiful wife, the rest of the time is ours. Let's treat this trip as though we were courting again."

"Like one long date. How wonderful. We haven't had special time together in a long time," said Kay.

"Maybe this job loss is a good thing from the standpoint of reevaluating what's important in life. Kay, sweetheart, I think we are both guilty of being in the rut of letting the cares and worries of this old world block out what's important—God, faith, family, and friends."

"Charles, my love, I think you're right."

They leaned back into the super soft seats and closed their eyes to relax. Soon, the train lurched forward. Charles and Kay placed a small CD player, with restful instrumental music turned on low, between them, and held hands as they watched the scenery go by.

"Look how beautiful," exclaimed Kay with awe.

"Hon, I'm so glad we're sharing this together."

Before they knew, it was time to meet others in the dining car. While they were waiting for the meal to be served, someone called, "Kay Kuntz? How are you?"

Kay turned to see an old high school classmate. "I'm good, but I'm married now. This is my husband Charles Johnson. Barb, it's been years. How are you doing?"

"Great, and this is my better half, Forest Dunham."

"Nice to meet you."

"We are on vacation to a place called Peaceful Valley Bed and Breakfast. Ever hear of it?" asked Barb.

"Yes, we're going there too," stated Kay.

Kay and Barb had a mini high school reunion while Charles and Forest talked sports and other guy stuff. Suddenly, the conductor raced into the car. "We just received an urgent weather bulletin over the radio. There is a massive storm system with several potential tornadoes. It's forty miles away but moving our way fast. We are ten miles from a large underground cave. It will be shelter for everyone if the storm is bad. The engineer is going to speed up to get there."

A mile before the cave, there was a loud clap of thunder as lightening stuck the top half of a hundred-foot-tall oak, sending the seventy-inch-diameter log onto the train track. The engineer barely avoided a derailment. Rain started just as everyone exited the train. They hurried in the direction of the cave.

Minutes later, torrents of wind-driven rain was now pelting everyone as they ran for cover. It felt like pins and needles on the skin. As the wind intensified and the lightening increased, the group found a big old concrete block building. It was an abandoned food warehouse. Charles asked Kay to stay with the others. She watched and waited patiently while Charles, Forest, and some other men managed to force the doors. Charles looked up to see a reinforced roof.

"The roof is good, but a strong tornado could turn tree limbs or other debris into concrete-penetrating missiles. Here's our answer," yelled Charles. The warehouse had a heavy all-metal cold storage area taking up about one half of the building. "Forest, help me break the lock so we don't get stuck in here after the storm. You other men hurry to get the crowd in here as swiftly and orderly as possible."

A few minutes later, Kay was at Charles's side. "Everyone is safely inside," she told him. A tree crashed through a window, and the howling wind became so strong it took several men to close the storage area and put up a barricade to block out the storm. The sound of an oncoming train could be heard outside along with loud cracking sounds. It seemed like an eternity as the strong tornado passed over.

Then an eerie calm settled in. The engineer said, "I think the storm is over. Let's open the doors and see."

Charles forcefully yelled, "Don't you dare touch those doors yet."

"It's over," said the engineer. "We need to get to the train to see if it is still functional. I have to radio headquarters and let them know everyone is safe and sound. Then we have to finish the trip."

"That's just the point—the first priority is everyone's safety. They told you on the train radio that there was potentially more than one tornado and they were large, right?" asked Charles.

"Yes. But it's over?"

"Not necessarily. There may be more than one tornado traveling together. Or if the funnel is large enough, we are in the eye—the calm of the storm—until we get the other side of it. It might even be stronger than what we have encountered so far."

"Are you a weatherman?" someone bellowed angrily from the group.

"No, but I used to work at a metal fabricating plant. A lot of times we had to make building parts for construction. Designs had to withstand storms. That's how I know."

"Well, I've got a schedule to keep, and these people have places they need to be," barked the engineer impatiently.

"He's right," called another voice from the sea of people. "Listen to him. Wait another thirty minutes—if more storms happen. And I am a meteorologist."

Before the engineer could answer, the sound of another rushing train could be heard. Only this time it also felt like an earthquake as the whole building shook. A few women screamed and children cried. Kay and Charles knelt and held hands.

Kay prayed, "Lord Jesus, as you were in a boat during a storm, calm the sea and stop the storm. In your name we ask you to stop the storm in our lives now. Amen."

They barely had spoken the words when the wind ceased. After waiting a while longer, no more storms.

The men moved the barricades and opened battered doors. Songbirds could be heard through many cracked and blown-out windows. Just as Charles predicted, the main roof supports held but sunlight was streaming through singles reminiscent of a slice of Swiss cheese. Large tree branches and other debris were through the walls and throughout most of the building.

Some of the crowd looked around the building with a look of horror on their faces. "If we had left earlier," said the engineer soberly, "many would have been hurt or dead."

The crowd thanked Charles and let out a cheer. "I really didn't do that much except use my experience as best as I could. But don't praise me. Praise God. I didn't know this old warehouse was here. But God did. And even though this building has been totaled, he kept everyone safe."

"You're right," called another voice as someone stepped from the crowd with a Bible. "I'm a pastor from a nearby town. I'm embarrassed to admit I should have stepped forward sooner to help somehow. But my wife is not well and had a panic attack. I have been an ordained minister for years, and this is the first miracle I witnessed. The church I grew up in taught that miracles happened in Bible days but don't happen that often today, if at all. I now know that thinking is wrong. Today showed me if you have faith in God, He still does miracles today. This has changed me forever as a person and a pastor." He led a prayer of thanksgiving.

Then the engineer shook Charles hand, "Please forgive me for being such a jerk?"

"Apology accepted—no hard feelings."

Kay and Charles helped gather the people to begin the walk back to the train. It was a slow process to traverse the obstacle course of tree limbs, debris, and big puddles and wet slippery terrain. It became a team effort as people helped each other. But as they got closer, the train fallen trees were fewer, and after several hours, the train passengers finally arrived back at the train.

Unbelievably, except for some broken and cracked windows in each car and the original fallen tree on the tracks, the train was safe and operable. The engineer used the radio to let headquarters know that everyone was all right and accounted for. He then requested a repair crew to fix the windows and a road crew to handle the log removal. Before nightfall, all the passengers had eaten and were resting, and the train was moving again.

Kay and Charles finally arrived at Peaceful Valley Bed and Breakfast. The rest of Kay and Charles trip went without incident.

A few days before their anniversary vacation ended, Charles told Kay, "I've got some news. When I checked my emails today, a company offered me a good job."

"That's great!"

"I have a job as a field manager for a chain of hardware stores. One problem though, I'll only be home on weekends."

"Oh my," said Kay.

"Honey, it's really good pay. I start out at a salary almost as much as the factory. I'll still keep looking for a good job that I can be at home."

"All right, Charles, I trust you to do what is best for the family."

4

Gentleman Farmer

Kay busied herself with ironing when Evie Grace skipped into the family room. Evie asked, "Mommy, is today Friday?

"Yes."

"Is Daddy coming home today?"

"Yes, honey, unless something happens at Daddy's work again. Remember, for weeks, he had to take over running a new store when the manager quit and the assistant manager needed additional training."

"I miss Daddy."

"I know you do, sweetheart. So do your sister and brother and I. Daddy will be home soon. Why don't you help me fold the towels while we are waiting for Susie and James to finish weeding the posy beds."

Just then, the phone rang. It was Charles. "Kay, it looks like I won't be home this weekend either. I'm sixty miles away. I've put so many miles on my car the fuel pump and universal joint went. Some of the parts aren't in stock. The mechanic cannot finish the car until Monday or Tuesday. I'm trying to find a rental car. If I locate one, I'll try to be home tonight."

"Keep us posted, dear," answered Kay as she tried her best to remain cheerful.

Later, Charles called with more bad news. "I got a rental, but my boss called with yet another business emergency. A different field manager, soon to be retiring, is in the hospital. A store that is in his territory is on the first floor of a two-story mall. There was a major water line break in the mall flooding the entire store. The boss needs me to meet with an insurance adjuster concerning damage inventory and shelving. He also wants me to meet with the owner of the mall and find a new location for the store as soon as possible.

"Kay, I know this stinks since I've been away so long. But because I'm the newest field manager hired, not only do I have my region, I also get stuck with the situations no one else wants. These crazy hours cannot go on forever."

Kay sighed in exasperation. "Charles, have you had any time to check on other job applications?"

"Barely—but nothing. I need to find a job that provides for the family."

"But, honey, what good is the job if you never get to see the family."

"I know what you mean, but I don't know what to do right now. Maybe the hours will improve."

"I hope you're right."

The next weekend came and still no Charles. Kay arranged on Sunday for a babysitter for a day and went to a ladies' retreat. While there, she met a lady from the Midwest. Her name was Marge. Marge happened to mention about a gentleman farmer that severely twisted his wrist and was in desperate need of someone that had experience on a dairy farm. She thought the job would last a minimum of six months to a year. Kay got the information.

After she arrived home on Monday, she phoned Thomas Greling to see if the position was still open. It was. Mr. Greling was impressed to hear that Charles had spent many summers as a kid on a relative's large dairy farm.

"I'm interested. Please have him give me a call as soon as possible."

Kay then checked if a school in the area had any openings. A kindergarten teacher was moving to another state. Kay quickly submitted her résumé. The school accepted her application on Tuesday to start in late August.

Once she realized that their lives were heading west, she wondered how to explain this to Charles. She hoped he would not be upset that her job search for both of them only took a couple days when he had been searching for months. *I hope I don't hurt his pride.* While Kay was getting up the nerve to call Charles, the phone rang.

It was her husband. "Honey, I had to quit my job. We are now at eight weeks since I've been home. Even with all the work I've done, my boss was upset when I went to pick up my car at the end of the day. On top of that, he wanted to give me the retiring field manager's area in addition to mine. He readily admitted that I would only get home for a couple days once only every six or nine months. I informed him that was not acceptable. My family is important to me. I asked him if I could just keep my existing region. The boss said no. He was cost cutting and merging both areas into one with a pay increase only a small amount above one area. I told him I would give him two weeks' notice. He was so angry he said, 'Leave now.' Kay, I said I quit. Please don't be upset with me."

"Charles, I think what you did was wonderful."

"Huh?"

Kay said, "We need you home. Last night when I put the girls to bed, little Evie asked me if you were ever coming home.

"Oh my," said Charles.

Kay said, "Charles, you forgot about putting your farming experience on your résumé."

"What?"

"You told me you enjoyed that remember?"

"Yes, but who needs an aging farm hand?"

"A gentleman farmer," answered Kay. She took a deep breath and told him everything about the jobs in the Midwest.

"Honey, I'll call the farmer, but I know the job won't pay enough to support the family and pay a mortgage—long term after severance pay from the factory is used."

"I had plenty of time to think this through. First, I feel like our future is in the Midwest. However, until we're sure, I'm taking a one-year sabbatical from my job here. Our church is hiring a youth pastor. The church cannot afford a big down payment on a second parsonage. They want to rent our house. The amount of rent the deacons want to pay will cover our monthly mortgage payment with a hundred dollars to spare. My new job will be considered full-time with full benefits including medical. But the hours are a little over four hours a day since it is kindergarten. The fewer hours mean no babysitter, and I'll be home before the bus drops the children home. Charles, if the farmer's job ends, I'm sure you will find a career. And best of all, we'll be together!"

"You're right. What is the farmer's number?"

Twenty minutes later, Charles called back. "I talked to Mr. Greling. The job not only includes a fair paycheck for the work but also includes lodging. Honey, it looks like we are heading west."

"Great."

One hour later, Charles was at the door with pizza and roses. Everyone was ecstatic, and the kids were excited about the move.

When they were in bed, Kay inquired, "Charles, you're not bothered that I had already looked into things about our new jobs?"

"Sweetheart, if I had been upset would, I have brought you roses? This worked out—that's all that matters. We'll have to decide what we are taking and get packed up. Thomas Greling is expecting us in about a week.

"That's not much time. Charles, you and James Robert will have to move the heavy stuff."

"Okay, but why?"

Kay took another deep breath. "Charles, I have another reason why the family needs you home. We are going to have another baby."

"Kay, that's wonderful. I should have brought two dozen roses." He gave her a hug.

Within a day, they packed up clothing, toys, computers, heirlooms, and some furniture. Since they were limited in time, when they left the house keys off with Pastor Evans, he was very happy.

Pastor Evans remarked, "When the finance committee heard that furniture is included too, they approved a fifty-dollar-a-month increase in the rent. We have your new address, and when it's time for the next rent check, we will mail it to you. But we are giving your rent in cash now." He handed them an envelope.

Kay and Charles opened the envelope. It was full of cash. "It's too much money," said a surprised Charles.

"Right now you guys have a long trip ahead. A car doesn't run on air, and meals and hotel add up. There is the added expense of the moving van and transport of Kay's car. At the prayer meeting last night, the congregation voted to give you three months of rent upfront." Also, Pastor Evans added, "Here is the telephone number of Pastor Jim Sands, the minister of your new church."

"Thank you so much," they said with a tearful goodbye.

Shortly before a week of traveling, Kay and Charles and the kids turned off the main road and onto the Greling farm road. They stopped in front of the old white farmhouse. Thomas Greling came out to meet them.

"You have perfect timing. I'll show you where the hands cottage is. The moving van arrived ten minutes ago. Pastor Sands, his wife, and a few other people from church are here to get you settled. While they are helping Kay and the kids, Charles, I'm behind with work. You need to start working immediately," said Thomas Greling gruffly.

"You got it," answered Charles cheerfully as Charles followed Thomas to the barn.

With the help from the new church members, Kay was surprised how quickly everything was totally set up. They even brought groceries.

"We also brought supper for all of us including Thomas. That will give us a chance to get to know each other." Pastor Sands added, "Thomas Greling is a good man, but he's rough around the edges and has lived alone a long time."

Kristen Sands said, "So if at times he seems short with you or Charles or the children, please don't take it personally."

"I'll keep that in mind," Kay said to the pastor's wife.

Later at the beginning of the meal in the small cottage, Thomas seemed like a fish out of water. During the dinner, someone mentioned about how hard it was for Thomas to stay in touch with Priscilla, his daughter, in Alaska.

"Mail takes too long, and she is an isolated area. Phones don't always work. She uses satellite for her computer. She bought me a computer, but I don't know anything about it."

"I'd be glad to help you. I can teach you how to use it, sir," offered James Robert.

"We'll see," mumbled Thomas Greling.

Kay also added, "Mr. Greling, I know it must be difficult to cook with that injured wrist. When I'm fixing supper for my family, I'll be happy to cook yours too. On days where you to just want to rest quietly, I'll gladly bring the meal over to your house. However, anytime you would like to join us, you are more than welcome."

"We'll see," grumbled Thomas with an ever so small smile.

"In addition to helping on the farm, if you need help with anything else, just ask," stated Charles.

"May be." Thomas nodded.

As the meal progressed, Kay thought Thomas's rough emotional exterior seemed to soften slightly.

Later, everyone was almost too keyed up to sleep. When Kay checked on the kids, she overheard Evelyn Grace and Susie Kay talking about Thomas.

Susie said, "I don't think Mr. Greling likes people much."

"No," said Evie. "I think I know what's wrong. His name is Thomas, right?"

"Yes," said Susie.

"Part of it is his first name."

"How?" asked Susie.

"Doubting Thomas," answered Evie emphatically.

"Evelyn Grace Johnson," said Susie Kay in a hushed shocked tone.

"Really, Mr. Greling doubts if people love him. We just need to show him he is loved."

"And how are we going to do that?" inquired Susie Kay.

"I don't know yet. I'll have to think on it."

Kay knocked on the girl's bedroom door. "Hey, you two, lights out and good night!"

5

Leaning on the Lord

Thomas Greling looked from the evening paper as Charles and Kay entered into his parlor and pulled the pocket doors closed. "We need to talk with you," Charles said as Kay sadly nodded in agreement. Thomas knew from their grim faces something was terribly wrong. Charles had mentioned Kay had an appointment with Dr. Hoffman that day.

"Is everything all right with the baby?" inquired Thomas.

"For now, but…" Charles's voice wavered as he tried to hide his fear.

Kay quietly added, "These last few months have been difficult. After reviewing the latest tests and ultrasound, the doctor feels that I should be admitted to a big hospital for the remainder of the pregnancy, so if anything goes wrong, help is there immediately to have a safe delivery."

Charles said, "Before today, we thought the baby would be full term. The due date was to be late January or early February. We had asked Sandy Peters from church to take care of the children. But she went back east before Thanksgiving to spend the holiday season with her daughter's family. She planned to be back home a few days after the New Year. Our families cannot travel this far. And the children are too young to go to their grandparents. We don't know who will take care of the family while we are at the hospital. Dr. Hoffman already made arrangements to have Kay admitted at City General the day after tomorrow."

Thomas cleared his throat and said, "Charles, you have been one of the best hands on the farm I've ever had. And even though James Robert is young, he is a respectful and hardworking teenager. Charles, you and I had already planned to have him fill in for you after school. So instead of a few days, he will be filling in for you longer. I'll help him—I have no problem with that at all. Right now you belong at Kay's side for however long it takes. I know the hands cottage is next door, but as you said, the kids are too young. This house is plenty big enough for four more people."

"Four more?" asked Charles and Kay.

"I'll ask my housekeeper, Widow Boyer, to move in—temporarily, of course—to help. I'm sure she will."

"Susie and Evie are younger. Evie can be an active five-year-old," exclaimed Kay. "Are you sure? She can be a handful at times."

"Oh, I'm sure. It's been far too many years since the voice of children has been heard in this house. Susie's personality is like my daughter's personality years ago. Tiny Evelyn Grace reminds me all too well of someone else I know." Thomas said with a twinkle in his eye. "I'm looking forward to it. Just don't let the kids know I said that."

"Thank you so much, Thomas. You have lifted one heavy concern off our shoulders," said Charles.

Thomas looked at Kay. "I know you're missing your family at a time when you need them the most. You guys have been so helpful to me. I hope you don't mind if I give some fatherly advice. Kay, it's over a month until Christmas and school vacation, and you and the kids have never been separated. But, Kay, you have to focus on your health and the life you carry. Stressing out over everything will not be good. You can stay in touch with the kids by phone and that darned newfangled Internet.

"Joyce Boyer is a very kind, loving person. She is also a great cook and baker. We'll give them the best Christmas ever and keep them busy. Then when Charles and you and the baby come home, we will have a second Christmas celebration. Just bring the kids tomorrow after school. I'll have everything ready. Now, Charles, I know there is a lot of packing for the kids and your trip to the hospital, but please take my advice. At noon tomorrow, take Kay out for a luncheon date to share time together before the hospital stay."

"I will," replied Charles.

"Good," said Thomas. "Then I'll see you tomorrow." After Charles and Kay left, he hurried to the telephone to call Joyce to ask her help.

After answering with a hearty hello, Joyce listened to Thomas. She answered, "Sure thing. Just one thing—I already planned to be with family on Christmas Eve and Christmas morning. I'll help you get dinner set up, and then I'll have to leave at noon on December twenty-fourth and I will be back before one on Christmas Day. *Tom, can you handle three kids on your own for twenty-four hours?*"

"Of course I can," barked Thomas. "It will be a piece of cake."

"Un huh," responded Joyce. "Well, I've got shopping to do. See you early tomorrow morning."

At 6:30 a.m., there was a knock at the door. Thomas opened the door to see Joyce with a big smile. She had multiple suitcases, heavy-duty vacuum cleaner, bags of cleaning supplies, groceries, boxes of Christmas decorations, and wrapping paper. She also had stuff for the kids—ribbon, construction paper poster board, glue, glitter, and other craft supplies.

"Charles and I just finished milking the cows," said Thomas.

Joyce said, "I'll make a big pot of coffee. After the first cup of coffee, Thomas, you strip the sheets and coverlet off all the beds while I mop the laundry room and kitchen. Then while the bedding is in the dryer, you wash the windows while I dust and vacuum. If everything goes as planned, we should be done with the upstairs before lunch. I'll start a big pot of chili and let it simmer on the back of the stove while we dust and vacuum downstairs."

"Charles and Kay are bringing the kids over at four," said Thomas.

"Good. That will give me plenty of time to make up the beds and mix up a couple of pans of cornbread before they arrive."

Thomas was helping Joyce set the table for seven when he looked out the window when he saw the school bus coming down the dusty lane. "They soon will be here."

"Don't worry, Thomas," exclaimed Joyce, "we still have twenty to thirty minutes before Charles and Kay bring the family over."

Later as the Johnson family opened the front door, the combined aroma of hearty chili and freshly baked cornbread wafted through the old farmhouse. Thomas escorted his visitors to the dining room and introduced Joyce Boyer to the family. During the meal, everyone laughed, joked, and got to know each other. Then after dessert, little Evie Grace looked over at her mother and started to cry.

"What's wrong?" implored Kay as she and Charles quickly went to her side.

Through great sobs, little Evie blurted out, "I know you said we will have a special vacation. But, Mommy, who will read me a story before bedtime while you and Daddy are gone?" Kay and Charles gave her a big hug.

James said, "It will be all right."

Susie added, "We're going to have a great time."

Joyce said, "We'll have a lot to do to get ready for Christmas and the baby. We'll be so busy time will fly, and your parents and the baby will be back before you know it."

"If you say so, I guess," answered Evie.

Then Thomas got up from the table. "Charles, you have stuff to do. Joyce, you and Kay clear the table." He said to the children, "You know I have a library upstairs. It has a lot of different kinds of books." He walked over to tiny Evie.

"How about we all play follow the leader?" As Thomas picked her up in his arms, she gave him a big smile and nodded yes. While Thomas and the children headed to the library, Charles quickly brought in the kids Christmas gifts and hid them in Thomas Greling's closet in the den. Kay helped Joyce take the dishes into the kitchen.

Joyce quietly reassured Kay. "Don't worry. Thomas and I will treat the children like they are our own kids. And we will be praying for Charles, you, and the baby," said Joyce as they hugged.

"Thank you."

Joyce added, "Before you leave, Charles is taking care of milking the cows. I can do the dishes myself. Evie Grace needs a little more time with you for this transition. Go upstairs and give Evie her bath, and then we'll both put her to bed."

"Good idea," replied Kay.

As Kay reached the top of the stairs, a happily excited Evie met her. "Mommy, Grandpa Tom helped me find a storybook."

"Really?"

"Right now he is showing James and Susie books and something called *encl*...something. It has a lot of info in it."

"Encyclopedia?" said Kay.

"Yeah, that's it. He said he will help us find a new book every night."

"That's great, but right now, it's time for your bath."

"Okey dokey," answered Evie.

A short time later, Thomas entered the bedroom. "Who wants to hear a bedtime story? I've got two books here. One for Evie and one for Susie.

"We do," shouted Evie and Susie.

Joyce said, "Also every night, I'm going to give you two hugs and two kisses—one hug and kiss is from me and one hug and kiss is from your parents."

Kay smiled and so did Susie.

Joyce added, "Now we thought Evie, you, and your sister would be happier in the same bedroom. But if either of you need me, I'm in the next room—just call me. James's room is beside Thomas's room. So everyone will have someone close by."

When the stories and bedtime prayers were over, Charles and James came in. Charles said, "James and I finished in the barn and the milking is done. We came in to say good night to the girls." Charles also hugged both of his daughters and gave them a tearful goodbye.

Thomas cleared his throat. "Before you know it, kids, your parents will be back home." Joyce turned off the bedroom light. Thomas continued, "Right now, Charles, you and Kay better get going. If you leave now, you can cover a lot of miles before you quit for the night. Then you won't have to push so hard tomorrow."

Thomas, Joyce, Charles, Kay, and James walked downstairs and out onto the front porch. Charles said, "You're a great son. We love you. Take care of your sisters. Thank you for helping Mr. Greling for me." Charles and Kay gave their son a bear hug.

"I will. I won't let you down let, you and Mom down," answered James Robert soberly.

Kay gently kissed James on the cheek. She said, "We are so proud of you."

"Don't worry, James is up to the job," said Thomas

"But we'll be helping hold the fort down," exclaimed Joyce.

After one last round of hugs, Charles and Kay began their long trip to City General Hospital.

6

Getting Ready

Thomas Greling and James finished hanging Christmas lights on the outside of the house and then put a massive star on the century-old weathered plank barn. As they put away the ladders, Joyce shouted out, "Okay, guys, time to stop a while. After all, even Santa and his elves take a break occasionally." Little Evie was intently listening to every word. The girls brought out a large tray of cookies and hot chocolate. Joyce poured the steaming hot chocolate in big mugs, Evie Grace tossed in miniature marshmallows, and Susie Kay added a peppermint candy cane for additional fun to each mug.

As Thomas neared the front porch, he called, "Susie, Evie, flip the porch switch and we'll see if the lights work."

"Oh, it's like a fairytale, Grandpa Tom!" exclaimed Evelyn Grace with a look of awe on her expressive face.

"It's beautiful," stated Susie with excitement as she passed out the hot chocolate.

"Great job," added Joyce. "Now relax before doing the milking. Enjoy the cookies."

"There are all different kinds to sample," said Susie.

"Grandma Joyce helped us make them," said Evie proudly. "What's your favorite?"

"They're all good," quipped James and Thomas as they reached for more.

"We are going to take several days and make candy and bake for Christmas," replied Susie. "Grandma Joyce said we'll make a lot and put it in the freezer so it's fresh for Christmas."

Joyce Boyer injected, "There will also be plenty of goodies put back for the second Christmas celebration when Kay, Charles, and the baby return."

After sampling the goodies and deciding what to make for Christmas, Joyce said, "Girls, please take the tray and mugs into the kitchen to wash. I need to talk to Thomas about something. I'll be in shortly to help."

"Sure thing," answered Susie, "come on, Evie."

James added, "I'll get the milking started," as he headed back to the barn.

"That's fine," replied Thomas. "What's up, Joyce?"

"We still need to keep the kids busy to keep them from worrying about their parents."

"I thought we were already doing that. What are you talking about, Joyce? You brought enough crafts and decorations to fill Santa's sleigh."

"Yes, right now I'm keeping the girls busy baking, candy making on weekends, and after homework on school nights. We started decorating the house. The girls are also in rehearsal the church Christmas pageant. But in ten days, Christmas vacation starts and they will have more time to think about Christmas without Mom and Dad. And it's not just two little girls. We have to plan so much to keep them so busy that they don't think about their missing loved ones."

"James Robert is doing well—but the longer the absence, he is old enough to realize the seriousness of Kay's condition. He's keeping that all in. Thomas, please see if you can get him to confide in you."

"I see what you mean now, Joyce. What do you have in mind?"

"Well, you just gave me the idea with James."

"I did?"

"Yes, when you said I brought a sleigh full of stuff. Thomas, do you still have that old sleigh covered in the barn?"

"I still have it, but it's in need of repair and a paint job."

"Perfect Christmas project for a teenage boy. Then at Christmas, we can have a sleigh ride. I know the girls and I would love it."

"You would, huh?" Thomas smiled.

"Okay." Joyce blushed. "Remember, while you and James are working on it, you can talk with him and give him the support he needs."

"I can do that. Anything else for Operation Busy Christmas?"

"Good title," quipped Joyce. "Yes, I jotted down a list today shortly before the kids came home from school."

"Well, let's have it. It's starting to get cold out here and the hot chocolate is wearing off."

Joyce quickly replied, "Here's the list. One, help the kids really decorate the house. Two, help the kids make gifts. Three, we can take the kids shopping and help them buy gifts they cannot make. Four, help them wrap gifts. Five, Thomas, I know you haven't had a tree in this house in years. But these children need it. Take a walk in the woods and have them pick a tree. Six, go to the Christmas pageant. Seven, caroling. Eight, lastly, before Christmas, the girls need a visit from someone dressed in red with a long white beard. I bought a suit in your size."

"Joyce Boyer, I've come to love these children and want them to have a great Christmas. I agree with everything on the list except the last one. No way are you getting me in a darn Santa suit!"

"Please think about it, Tom. It would mean so much to the girls and me," pleaded Joyce.

"I'll gladly help with all the items except the last one. I've got to help James in the barn."

Thomas trudged to the barn muttering, "Santa suit, indeed," as he went. He shoved the barn door so hard it creaked, sounding like it was coming off its hinges. Thomas grabbed the door pulling it back to its proper position. He was feeling embarrassed by his anger when he saw a very startled and fearful boy looking back at him. "Boy, you're not afraid of me, are you? I had something on my mind and did not realize how hard I hit the door."

"You just surprised me, that's all," said James bluntly as he quickly moved his hand over his face but not quickly enough.

Thomas saw an unmistakable tear going down the lad's face as James suddenly turned away. "Son, we need to talk," said Thomas as he firmly touched James Robert's shoulder and gently turned him around. "What's wrong, James?"

"Dad said to take over and do his work for you while they're gone. I really want to do it. On Saturday, I can work a full day. On Sunday, a partial day because of church and rest. During the week since there is school and homework, I can only work a few hours each day. I feel I'm letting you down as well as my promise to Dad. I'm trying to watch my sisters to make sure their morale is up. Then today my parents' phone call to us really scared me.

"Susie and Evie are too young to really understand what could happen to Mom or the baby. I've known Mom and Dad long enough to know when I hear stress and worry in their voices. They're trying their best to hide it. But I can tell. I don't want anything to happen, but if something happens to the baby or Mom, how do I help the family? I know I should be here, but I can't help feeling like I should be at the hospital too to support them. I don't know what to do. While I was out here working alone, I was also praying for an answer."

Thomas inquired, "And did God answer?"

"No! What am I doing wrong? I thought I should quit school until my parents are back so I can work full-time for you."

"Nonsense, I will not let you become a high school dropout before you even start middle school!"

James Robert fell to his knees in tears. Thomas knelt by James and pulled into his arms. "Let it out, son. Let it out! You're worrying way too much about so many things. You are not doing anything wrong. My dearly departed wife, Hattie, was always closer to the Lord than me. She always said, 'If while praying to the Lord about worry or problems, you have to give it to him and let go of the worry.' If you are still concentrating on the problem, you're never going to be able to hear his answer."

"Really?" asked James Robert.

"Really, you have to calm down and get quiet to hear him and give him time to work it out. That was one principle my Hattie lived by. James, as far as stepping into your dad's shoes while he is gone is limited. You cannot carry the concerns of the whole family on your twelve-going-on-thirteen-year-old shoulders. Remember, your dad is the head of the family. Above him is the Lord.

"I'll let you in on a little secret. You know I have my daughter Priscilla and her family that I love, but I always hoped that Hattie and I could have had a son. Charles, your dad is the kind of man I would be proud to call son. And since I consider him a son, that means James you are a grandson. So, grandson, you are doing a wonderful job!"

"You mean it?" asked James. "Sometimes when we were working together, you seemed so stern or displeased."

"I wasn't displeased with you or the quality of your work. Sometimes I have stuff on my mind and am set in my ways, that's all."

"Oh, I understand now," said James.

"Come on, grandson, I want to show you something."

"Great," said James with a big smile on his face.

Thomas walked over to a corner of the large barn and lifted a tarp. Under the tarp was an old sleigh. "What do you think of making this a project for Christmas?" James nodded an enthusiastic yes. "If we both work on it, together we should be able to give Joyce and your sisters a sleigh ride before Christmas. I bought some paint and black Rust-Oleum for the runners. "Let's get the chores done and we'll have a little time to start to sand the sleigh before bedtime."

"Let's do it," exclaimed James Robert.

They finished the chores quickly and started working on their secret Christmas project.

7

Countdown to a Miracle

"Come on, girls, you slept in. This is the last of school before Christmas vacation. Thomas and James already ate. Get dressed by the time you come down, and I'll have breakfast ready." Joyce added, "Remember, you only have half a day. Don't get on the bus since I'll be picking you up at school. There is the final rehearsal for the Christmas pageant this afternoon. And then we are going Christmas shopping for your parents, brother, and Grandpa Thomas. Then we will meet up with James and Thomas at the Country Café for supper before coming home."

"Okey dokey, Grandma Joyce," said Evie.

Later as the girls grabbed their lunches and headed for the door, Joyce handed them boxes of cupcakes. "Don't forget the goodies we made for your class Christmas parties."

"Thank you," called the girls in unison as they raced to get on the bus.

"Come on, what's keeping you two? The bus driver can't wait forever," scolded James.

"We're coming," said Evie.

Susie answered, "I'm walking as fast as I can. Evie has the book bags, and I'm carrying three boxes of Christmas cupcakes. Here, James Robert, take your box now."

"Okay, sis, okay!" said James as he helped his sisters on the bus.

They waved goodbye to Joyce and Thomas as the bus rolled down the lane.

"Come on, Thomas, I've got hot coffee. Do you want a cup or two?" inquired Joyce.

"Sure," answered Thomas. "This will be our last chance to discuss things and make any last-minute changes to Operation Busy Christmas. Last week, we took the kids caroling. James took his computer along to record it for Charles and Kay. He found a business in town to professionally copy it. James and I will pick it up today when we do our shopping before meeting up at the café."

Joyce said, "Tomorrow is December 23."

"I know," Thomas said. "What's left on the list? Or needs added? What's your battle strategy?"

"Battle strategy?" Joyce looked surprised. "We aren't at war."

"I beg to differ," said Thomas. "Joyce, you and I are fighting off sadness, worry, and the kids' homesickness for their parents."

"Oh," she said, "well, how are we doing?"

"Good so far," answered Thomas.

"One, decorate the house—almost done. Seven, caroling, done," said Joyce.

"Three, shopping, we're doing it today," stated Thomas.

Joyce added, "I have to finish the nut rolls. So don't forget to pick up our gifts for the children. I already have them on lay away at these stores. She handed him the necessary paperwork. Make sure you pick the gifts up and get them back here before you get James from school to maintain secrecy."

"Yes, sir. General Joyce, what's next?" Thomas questioned as he gave Joyce a smile and hearty salute.

Joyce laughed and said, "Quit kidding around. There is still a lot to do. How's the sleigh coming? Will it be ready in time?"

"Yes, James and I thought we would take everybody for a sleigh ride in the afternoon on Christmas Day.

"Great!"

Thomas said, "We should add things for between Christmas and New Year's."

"I guess you're right," answered Joyce. "Like what?"

"Teach the kids how to skate and ice fishing."

"Good the ideas are added. Now let's get back to the immediate list," stated Joyce. "Thomas, tomorrow morning, December 23, take the kids out in the woods and get the tree. I'll stay behind and wrap the children's gifts and cook lunch. Noon is lunch. Then set the tree up. But Thomas we'll leave the decorating of the tree until Christmas Eve day. One through three o'clock begin craft gifts. Four is supper, and then go to church for the Christmas pageant. December twenty-fourth—finish the gifts and kids wrapping the gifts and decorate the tree. Thomas, remember, I'm leaving before lunch on December twenty-fourth to spend Christmas with my family. I'll be back by one in time for Christmas dinner here."

"I know," said Thomas quietly, and a look of sadness came across his face as he stared into his coffee cup.

"I'll have a big casserole in the frig for Christmas Eve dinner. Just put it in the oven for forty-five minutes. Don't forget the candlelight service at church is at seven thirty that night."

"I can handle it."

"Thomas, will you reconsider item eight on my original list."

"Joyce, I'm not going to put on a beard and red flannel pajamas. That's it. End of subject!"

"Okay, okay." Joyce glanced at the kitchen clock. We have to get our track shoes on or our list will mean nothing. I've got a date with nut rolls, and you have to leave now to get to town to pick up the gifts. Get back here and hide them. Then get back to town for James Robert. Remember to be at the café at six. As soon as the nut rolls come out of the oven, I have to hit the road to pick up the girls for the rehearsal. "Let's get going."

"Yes, ma'am. General Joyce, sir, I'll follow your command." Thomas gave another salute.

"Oh, brother, get to town," said an exasperated Joyce Boyer with a smile.

Later while eating supper at the Country Café, it gave everyone a chance to rest from the day's hectic schedule. "Is everyone ready for Christmas?" asked Thomas and Joyce at almost the same time.

The children smiled at each other and answered, "We think so."

Little Evie Grace spoke up. "I've been thinking about something a lot."

"I hope it's something good or important, little sis," stated James.

Susie said, "James Robert, give her a chance."

"Okay, Susie."

"What's on your mind, Evie?" questioned Thomas.

"We celebrate Christmas as Jesus's birthday. Right?"

"Yes," said Joyce. "Remember how Pastor Sands explained that Jesus always has existed along with Father God and the Holy Spirit but came down from heaven to be our savior when we believe in him. He left heaven and was born in Bethlehem. We honor him by celebrating his earthly birth at Christmas and his saving us at Easter.

"Well, we are shopping and making gifts for everyone. When we were in the stores, I saw a lot of things on sale. But where were the signs for gifts for Jesus? I know only little words. Did I miss the signs for Jesus? Before Santa Claus delivers gifts to the children of the world, does he take his sleigh up to heaven and give Jesus his birthday gift first? If he doesn't—he should."

"Wow, that's a lot to think about," stated a very surprised Thomas. "Evelyn Grace as a five-year-old, you are too young to fully understand Jesus's gift of salvation. That God will show you at the right time. At a time when a lot of saved and unsaved get caught up totally in the world's planning only, they forget Jesus is the reason for the season. Little one, you get how important knowing Jesus is— when many adults will never get it until it's too late."

"What do you want to do, Evie Grace?" asked James Robert. "Can I help in any way?"

"I want to give Jesus a birthday cake," stated Evie in a matter-of-fact way. "And I want to invite him to dinner Christmas Eve."

Thomas almost choked on his coffee. "Honey, you realize he's in heaven now. How are you going to invite Jesus to dinner?"

"Easy. James, Susie, you remember Aaron Fisher and his family from back home."

"Yes, they're Jewish," said James. "They performed a Passover Seder ceremony at church."

"Ah huh. James, who was the old guy in the Bible that they set a place at the table for?"

"Elijah."

"That's who."

"And the family lets the door unlocked for him to come," added Susie.

"That's exactly what we'll do," a very excited Evelyn Grace exclaimed and smiled from ear to ear.

"Well, it looks like we will be baking a birthday cake when we get home," said Joyce.

"It seems that will be the case," responded Thomas.

"We can all join in helping make the best birthday cake ever," chimed in Susie Kay and James Robert.

"I'm sure it will be special no matter what," said Joyce.

"There's a lot to do tonight, so we better get going after dessert," stated Thomas firmly.

8

Seeing God at Work

While at the hospital

"Mr. and Mrs. Johnson, we have some wonderful news," said Dr. Mason. "When I checked the latest ultrasound, you are having twins. I think the second baby didn't show up on earlier tests because one is positioned under the other. The technician who performed this test at a slightly different angle. That's when the second fetus became visible."

"That's great," Charles exclaimed.

"Can you tell the sexes yet?" Kay asked.

"One is a girl. We cannot tell the sex of the other one yet. Both appear to be healthy. But we still have to keep a close watch on things. Dr. Hoffman was right when he diagnosed preeclampsia. The heavy swelling in your hands and feet is greatly reduced. Even though, Kay, your blood pressure and lab results are not the same for a typical pregnancy, they have improved since you were admitted. These weeks of mandatory bed rest have greatly increased the twins' changes of being born closer to term.

"My colleagues and I all feel the babies will be born premature. But the longer the time we get the better. Obviously, the closer we get to your due date, the health concerns for the twins diminish. We'll keep watching your blood pressure that it doesn't raise to anything like 140/90. Or, Kay, if you start having blurred vision, see flashing lights, unexpected pain or nausea let us know right away."

"I will," responded Kay.

"Good," said Dr. Mason, "I'll send the nurse in to get another urine sample to check for protein. While the nurse is doing that, how's the proud papa doing?"

The doctor asked Charles, "How about a cup of coffee?"

"Okay."

"How's the long-term job search coming?" the doctor asked as they walked out of Kay's room. Dr. Mason walked with Charles to the doctor's lounge. Charles talked about the latest news in job opportunities.

Once they reached the lounge, the doctor motioned to Charles to have a chair. "Do you take sugar or cream in your coffee?"

"No, I take it black—nothing in it. I like it strong," stated Charles.

"Then you'll love this then. Hospital coffee is so strong this stuff could walk. How about joining me in a doughnut too? It's been a long afternoon. We'll need to offset the coffee."

While they talked, Dr. Mason said, "I wanted to speak to you without Kay hearing this."

"You said in my wife's room that her condition had improved. It *has* improved?"

"Yes, but we're not out of the woods yet. I want you to be aware of the dangers." He then told Charles, "The nurses will closely monitor blood pressure, but there is a risk of seizure. I'm not saying it will definitely happen, but if it does, don't buzz the nurses' station. Hit the emergency button above Kay's bed. The other patient in your wife's semiprivate room is going home today. I'm going to authorize that another lady is not to be placed in the room until Kay delivers."

"Then you think she will go into labor soon."

"Yes. We'll put a cot in her room for you to be with her all the time. So she won't be suspicious, we'll just say that the hospital cares about your financial situation. The hospital wants you to save on hotel costs, hence the cot.

"Again, a seizure would be rare, but any sudden symptoms could mean we have to act promptly to ensure the safety of both mother and babies. I hope the preeclampsia doesn't worsen, but if it does, Kay's health could deteriorate rapidly until the birth and even possibly after."

"I'll be carefully watching Kay for any of the symptoms you mentioned, Doctor."

"Just one thing, Charles, can you observe for symptoms without letting her know. We don't want her stressing about health—it could make it worse."

"Yes, Dr. Mason," said Charles solemnly.

"Charles, don't get stressed out yourself. Remember, you're not alone in this, and Kay's pregnancy is further along. All the other doctors I've conferred with believe Kay will go into labor in early January if not before.

"I know you haven't done that much job searching since you left your computer at the hotel. I believe one of the best things you can do for Kay right now is to give her a project. The busier her mind, the less time to think about being in the hospital or being separated from the rest of the family.

"Please bring your computer and phone charger to the hospital. You can run them from Kay's room. The electric they use is minimal. Get a big notebook and have Kay keep track of it all."

"I'll do just as you say, Doctor."

"Good, good, my hope is she will be so occupied and relaxed that the babies will be here before you know it! Well, I have to get back to my rounds, and you need to get back to Kay before she wonders why you were gone so long."

"You've got that right, Dr. Mason. Thanks, I hope the rest of your day goes well," Charles said as he hurried back to Kay.

Luckily, Charles found Kay asleep. Charles thought, *Maybe she won't realize how long I've been with the doctor.* Just as he entered the room, she opened her eyes and sat up.

"What did Dr. Mason want?"

"To save us money, he wants me to move in with you and sleep on a cot. Honey, do you think you can put up with me all day?"

"Yes, of course. But are you sure it's just for financial reasons?" she said with questioning look on her face.

"Well, I have to admit, he did mention that he did not want you dwelling on being away from the kids. Besides, I could use your help in finding a permanent occupation when Thomas Greling's job is finished. We can work on it together—two heads are better than one."

"Charles, I'll gladly help you—but are you telling me everything?"

"Really, honey. I think you have been thinking too much. We'll make it a project. Whenever a nurse or doctor comes in or you have a test, get tired, or feel sick, we stop. After all, your health comes first. But you have to admit it, will get your mind off being in here."

"That's true enough. When do we start?"

"Tonight, when I go back to the hotel, I'll pack up. Then I'll stop by a dollar store get a big notebook, pens, and a few folders. Tomorrow when I become your roommate, we'll start right after nurses' rounds and breakfast."

"All right, let's do it!" Kay exclaimed as a smile spread across her face.

The next morning, bright and early, Charles moved into Kay's room. He also gave her an oversized notebook and small folding file. Within a few days, they had recorded all valid email addresses and phone numbers. Kay also catalogued all jobs by career or field.

Kay said, "There are over several hundred—no wonder you were going nuts trying to keep track of all of this."

"I didn't realize I had so much info. I just thought the more opportunities I accumulated, the greater my chances of finding the perfect position."

Then they started the long process to contact business owners to contact business owners to see which of the most promising jobs were still available. One afternoon, Charles and Kay had whittled the companies down to fifty with only a handful of personnel managers saying they might have openings in the next couple months.

"Now what?" said Charles.

Just then, Kay's phone rang. "Is this Kay Johnson?"

"Yes."

"I'm Pam Bender, the manager of the Peaceful Valley Bed and Breakfast. I've been trying to reach you for a while. I reviewed numbers on your reservation paperwork and talked to your relatives. They told me you were in the hospital and gave me your cell number."

"I just turned my phone on."

"I hope you get out of the hospital soon, but I'm actually calling about a job for your husband. Is he still looking?"

"Yes, he is."

"He worked in fabrication?"

"Right," both Charles and Kay exclaimed.

"Well, remember months ago when the two of you were en route here and the train ride was held up by horrendous weather?"

"We'll never forget," replied Charles.

"There was a man on the train that really was impressed by the way you handled things. His name is Allen Anderson. He's setting up a fabrication business close to where you now live. He has been looking for someone that has the right skills."

Charles quickly contacted Allen Anderson.

"Wonderful, I had almost given up hope of finding you, and then my wife recalled your wife saying you were traveling to the bed and breakfast. Not only do you have experience in the type of work but you exhibited something even more valuable—*firm leadership under pressure with compassion*. You are the perfect person for helping me get this venture started.

"I want you to meet the people I'm buying the equipment from. They will call me as soon as they are in the state. I realize you have to be with your wife. Can we have a short meeting at the hospital?"

"We'll have to clear it with the doctors, but I think we can."

A week later, Allen Anderson walked into Kay's room. Dr. Mason had previously ordered Charles cot moved out for a few hours and a folding table and chairs put in its place. The nurse had also brought in fresh coffee and doughnuts. Allen Anderson introduced himself and handed Kay a small package.

"It's just a little something for the babies. It's also great to formally meet you two."

"Thanks for the gift. And it's great to meet you too."

"I originally wanted you to take a look at the equipment pictures and give me your opinion on value. Because I'm still negotiating a purchase price with the owners. After talking to the owners, I found out that you have personal knowledge of the equipment."

"I do? That would mean after moving across the country, I'll be working with equipment from my old employer?" said a very surprised Charles.

Just then, David and Martin Logan walked into the room. "Charles, it's great seeing you again," said the Logans as everyone shook hands. After a short twenty-minute meeting, Martin Logan spoke up, "Mr. Anderson, since you are bringing Charles into this, we are willing to give you a great deal on the equipment. You said, Allen, you could not pay full value of the equipment with building costs, transport costs of equipment, installation, and working capital. You showed some contracts lined up. But without equipment, everything falls through. But as we had already discussed earlier about the business being a partnership with two partners. You and Charles."

"I thought that I would be a supervisor. I have money left from my severance pay, but it's not nearly the thousands needed to invest in this kind of business."

David Logan handed Kay a gift box as well. "It's for the babies too," he said and laughed as his dad, Martin Logan, continued.

Martin Logan added, "Allen, Charles, you know I am a businessman that looks at the bottom line. Charles, not only did you get the equipment dismantled quickly but we found out the last few days you had the dismantle team paint what needed painted and had minor maintenance done. You also put in a request to have new blacktop for the whole parking lot and new landscaping. Which we did. Because of what you did, we received an unbelievably high price for the building. We tried to find you to say thank, you but you and your family were already gone.

"Also, Charles, your years of experience and business knowledge is equivalent to money. Charles, Allen brings in money, building, some contracts, and limited experience for his 50 percent. Your 50 percent is first your experience. Second, you can hire the dismantle team to rebuild the equipment for quicker start up. Also a large number of our repeat customers have not found another company they are happy with. We feel obligated to help them also. Charles, we will connect them with you. That means this new business will start out with a client base as large as an ongoing business. Lastly, the equipment."

"I have to admit, this sounds great, but I still cannot afford to buy equipment unless I go to a bank."

"Charles, you don't need a bank. What's in your pocket?"

"Huh, two twenty-dollar bills?"

"Give me one of them and Merry Christmas. Charles, you just bought all the equipment. Not only did you make us money on the building but you're saving us a bundle on storage costs," said Martin Logan.

David Logan stepped forward and said, "We have to catch a plane soon, and Kay must be getting tired. Here is the contract. I also collected our customer list. Allen, you already arranged for shipment of the equipment. Allen and Charles, let's get things signed."

"Great."

Allen Anderson was the last one to leave. "Welcome, partner, I could not have done this without you. The building is an old warehouse five miles from where you live. It will provide a lot of jobs to the area. If you still want to help on the farm, you can. Sometimes you'll be able to work from home too.

"We'll be starting February first. So you can stop thinking about job searching and concentrate on taking care of Kay. I'll call you after the first of the year. Merry Christmas and Happy New Year, partner. Goodbye. Until then."

"Wow, Kay, are we dreaming or did this really happen?"

"It really happened, hon. Before all this started, all you wanted to do is what you loved doing for years. You will be but at an owner's pay. Praise the Lord, no more stressing on finances. Charles, do you want to call the kids tonight?"

"Kay, are you okay?"

"Yes, I'm just really very tired. I'm elated this happened, but maybe it's too much excitement."

"Kay, I'm going to buzz the nurse so she can check your vitals."

The nurse came in and checked Kay over. "The blood pressure was up a little but still within safe levels. I'll let the doctor know how tired she is. I'll also have an orderly remove the table and chairs and bring the cot back." Later she returned and said, "The doctor will come in the morning but he feels that both of you should rest now. I'll put the lights out and bring something light for supper later."

As Charles lay there listening to Kay's breathing as she slept, he also heard the muffled sounds of the hospital PA system calling different doctors and people walking in the hall. Charles prayed, *Thank you for the business opportunity, but send angels to watch over Kay.*

9

The Guest of Honor

Meanwhile back at the farm

As Thomas and James finished the evening milking upon returning from the Country Café, they anxiously entered the kitchen. "Is the special birthday cake baked yet?" asked Thomas.

"Yes," answered Joyce. "It's on a rack cooling. But we have a big problem."

"Did the cake burn?" joked Thomas.

"No. It's not the cake. While the cake was baking, I helped the girls get ready for bed. Then the plan was to have everyone decorate the cake before calling it a night. Evie Grace is all upset."

"Oh," Thomas said. "She finally realized that Jesus will not be here in person tomorrow night."

Joyce shook her head. "I think she's more excited about Christmas Eve dinner than anything Santa could bring her. She also informed me that if Jesus comes, she is going to ask him to bring her parents and the baby home for Christmas."

"Oh my goodness." James Robert gasped.

Joyce added, "She is happy about tomorrow. In her mind, the cake and inviting Jesus solves the problem of wanting to give Jesus a gift. In fact, Susie and Evie said their prayers early. Evie formally invited Jesus to his birthday supper during her prayers."

"So what has her so upset, then?" inquired Thomas.

"She actually had a worry list of three things. First was giving Jesus a gift, second wanting the whole family together for Christmas—both resolved by the birthday dinner and asking Jesus about missing family members. It's her third concern. At her class Christmas party, a classmate who had moved tolc her about lost mail and gifts until his parents filed a change of address with the post office. Remember, she is only five and a half.

"She is upstairs crying inconsolably because she forgot to put a change of address in her letter to Santa Claus. I had to get the cake out before it burned. Susie is with her now. I don't know what to do."

Thomas cleared his throat. "I'm afraid I do." Thomas turned to James. "If asked about a short period of time tonight, pretend I had additional stuff to do in the barn."

"All right, but why?" questioned James Robert.

"I think she needs a visit from Santa to set things straight."

"Are you sure?" inquired a shocked Joyce.

"I don't chew my cabbage twice. Yes. Joyce, where in the heck are those flannel pajamas?"

"In a box on the top shelf of the closet in the den. There is also a red bag of small toys and trinkets at the back of the closet."

"When I'm done, I'll leave the suit in the barn. Joyce, when we go into the woods tomorrow to get the tree, get it and put the suit away. The girls are bright—I don't want them to figure it out and spoil the whole thing."

"I'll take care of it," answered Joyce with a tear in her eye.

"Give me twenty minutes to change, put my clothes in a plastic bag, grab the gift bag, and get on the back porch. Then bring the girls down."

"You got it," said Joyce and gave Thomas a salute. As the clock hit twenty minutes, Joyce called the girls to come down and see the cake.

"We're coming, Grandma Joyce," said Susie Kay.

"How are you doing, Evie?" asked Joyce.

"I'm not sure," answered Evie as the sisters walked into the kitchen. Evie smiled slightly when she saw the lightly golden brown cake rounds cooling on the counter.

"Everything will work out, Evelyn Grace," stated Joyce in comforting tone.

"I hope," said Evie and gave a little sigh.

"We're all supposed to help decorate the cake," said Susie. "Where is Grandpa Thomas?"

"He said he had other things to do in the barn and will be in later," answered James.

Just then, there was a knock at the door. Joyce opened it.

"Ho ho. Merry Christmas."

"Oh my!" exclaimed Susie.

"It's Santa. He found us after all," Evie shouted with glee.

"I heard there are good children living here. Sometimes I personally check out addresses before my annual ride."

"Really?" questioned Evie her face a glow with happiness.

"Santa, will you help us decorate Jesus's birthday cake?" inquired Susie.

"Sure," stated Santa.

James Robert grinned. "Santa, Joyce, look up. You're both standing under mistletoe," exclaimed James.

"That wasn't there an hour ago," Joyce remarked.

"Oh, come on." Santa gave Joyce a quick peck on the cheek. Joyce smiled and blushed.

Little Evie scolded, "James, you're going to get Santa in trouble with Mrs. Claus."

"We better get back to the cake," stated Susie.

Once the cake was finished, Santa passed out the gifts. "I have to leave now. One of the elves is waiting with my sleigh down the road."

"Thanks, Santa. Merry Christmas to you and Mrs. Claus," said Susie and Evie in unison.

Santa waved and headed down the lane.

"Wow, what a visit. Who wants hot cocoa before bed?" inquired Joyce.

"We do," shouted the three children.

As Joyce stood at the stove stirring the cocoa, Thomas walked in.

"I just finished looking in on Mariah the mare. Did I miss anything?"

Evelyn Grace piped up, "Grandpa Thomas, Santa was here."

"Really?"

"Yes, he even helped with the cake," Susie chimed in.

"You don't say? It looks like I missed a lot?"

"We can all talk about as we sit down and enjoy cookies and cocoa," ordered Joyce.

The next morning before the kids were awake, Thomas and Joyce had one last Operation Busy Christmas meeting. "The Santa suit is in a big plastic bag behind a bale of hay."

"I'll get it," Joyce stated. "Also, while you and the kids get the tree, I'll make the casserole for tomorrow tonight. I'll have a post a note on it. Because I will also have Christmas dinner in the freezer and some containers in the frig. Within a half an hour after getting back early Christmas afternoon, we will eat."

"Okay," acknowledged Thomas. "The kids' gifts are in my den closet and your bedroom closet, right?"

"Yes, they will all be wrapped. Don't forget the candlelight service at seven thirty. After church, Thomas, all you need to do is help the kids decorate the tree and get the children to bed. Then quietly get the gifts under the tree. Lastly, get your rest and I'll see you on Christmas."

"I can handle it," Thomas told Joyce.

"I just wish I could be here to help you with Evie Grace's birthday gift for Jesus."

"You surely don't expect Him to come to supper. Do you, Joyce?"

"Christmas is a time of miracles. I don't know what to think. But if somehow the guest of honor does visit, I hope he likes baked macaroni and cheese. Remember, Evie will want to stay and wait for Jesus but be gently firm. You have to get an early start to town to get to church. The weather may be a good thing—a good excuse to leave. I had the radio on before you came down. They are calling for heavy snow and possible icy roads. Thomas, please be careful. You and the kids stay safe," implored Joyce.

"You worry too much," answered Thomas. "I'll drive carefully. But if the weather turns nasty, Joyce, please make sure you take care of yourself until you come back to me—ah, I mean, us."

"I will," Joyce promised with a tear in her eye.

Suddenly, the kids came bounding down the stairs. "What smells so good?" they shouted.

"The sausage, egg, and hash brown breakfast casserole is about ready."

Thomas said, "Robert, as an early Christmas gift to you, I already did the milking. We're all going to take the time for a good filling breakfast before marching into the woods to find the perfect tree. We can take the time to talk about anything." A lot of the discussion was about unfinished surprises and the children's excitement of their first ever tree hunting excursion into the woods.

"Grandpa Thomas, will Mommy and Daddy be here for Christmas?" asked Susie.

"I don't think so," answered Thomas.

"Susie, remember," Joyce said as she gently squeezed Susie's hand, "we will have the second Christmas once Kay, Charles, and the baby come home—no matter when. We'll just keep their gifts back and there are plenty of holiday goodies in the freezer. But to keep the Christmas cheer is all the more reason to celebrate the season to the fullest. Okay, everyone?"

Susie said, "You're right."

"Let's make it the best ever," chimed in James and Thomas.

"Okey dokey, Grandpa Thomas and Grandma Joyce." By the end of the meal, everyone was smiling.

Thomas said, "Hey, Joyce, hold down the fort. Get busy cooking for Christmas."

Thomas got started on their task. "The last one to the truck gets coal for Christmas," he called as he gathered the saw, ax, shovel, and coca in an extra-large thermos.

Evie Grace asked, "Grandpa Thomas, are you going to give yourself a lump of coal?"

"It might happen," Thomas answered as he tossed the tools into the truck bed of the old, battered red Ford pickup and climbed into the driver's seat.

As they strolled through the woods, they happily sang Christmas songs while searching for the perfect Tannenbaum. After a few hours and a spirited snowball fight later, the cheerful group found their evergreen. Thomas and James hoisted the eight-foot spruce into the truck and headed home. They set the tree up and ate lunch.

While everyone was working on gift projects, Joyce called, "Time to get dressed for church before supper."

Then they were on the road to church. The church was packed, and the children's pageant was a rousing success.

The next day before they knew it, it was time for Joyce to leave. They wished her an early Merry Christmas and began completion of last-minute gifts. Later, Thomas put the enormous casserole in the oven and set the timer.

Thomas asked Susie, "If James and I are still in the barn when the buzzer goes off, just shut the oven off. Will you girls be okay by yourselves while we are in the barn?"

"We'll be fine," answered Susie.

"While you are gone, Susie and I are going to finish your gift, Grandpa Thomas."

"Evelyn Grace Johnson, really?" exclaimed Susie.

"Well, we are. So what's the big deal?" answered Evie.

Thomas and James hurried through the chores and finished the final touches on the sleigh. The snow started to fall as they went back into the house. Susie and Evie had the table set and food ready.

Evie spoke up, "Remember, I put an extra chair. Can we wait a few minutes for Jesus?"

Thomas said, "James, just put the dinner rolls in the oven. They will take ten to twelve minutes. Once the bread is done, we are eating—guest of honor or no guest of honor."

"But, Grandpa Thomas, you're talking about Jesus the Son of God," stated Evie.

"I know, but take my word for it, Evie, Jesus loves you and loves everyone in the whole world from the beginning of time on. That's why he went to the cross. He gave his life to save people from sin."

"What is sin, Grandpa Thomas?"

"Evie, you are a little too young to fully understand. But sin is anything that is wrong or hurts others or yourself. Jesus went to the cross for everyone—but only people who admit wrong and believe he is the only Son of God will receive his gift of eternal life. Many people think they can get into heaven without doing that. But, Evelyn Grace, it's like if someone wants to give you a gift: you have to accept the gift. If you don't accept the gift from the giver, you don't get it. In life, if people don't accept Jesus, admit wrong, and ask him to live in their hearts, He's not going to accept them later."

"Oh, I think I understand now," said Evie.

"Evie, Jesus already knows how much you love him. You and Susie and James have worked hard on His birthday cake. He knows it. If He doesn't come in person, He still loves you!"

"That's right," said Susie and James.

Susie added, "I do not remember if I ever asked Jesus to forgive me. James, did you?"

"At church, a couple of years ago."

Evie said, "Sis, why don't we do it together?" Susie nodded. "Grandpa Thomas, how do we do this?"

"Just say what you feel in your heart."

"Grandpa Thomas, will you help us?"

"Okay. Please forgive my sin and wrongs. Jesus, I know you are God's son. Come into my life. Thank you. Amen."

As the two sisters repeated Thomas's prayer, both girls had big smiles.

"Is that it, Grandpa Thomas?"

"Did you mean what you said?"

"Yes."

"That's all there is to it," said Grandpa Thomas.

James Robert said, "Mom and Dad will be so happy. What a Christmas gift for them."

Thomas dapped his eyes with his bandana and cleared his throat. He looked out the window. "The snow is steady. Let's say grace and eat." Evie kept gazing at the door.

She asked, "Isn't rude to eat before Jesus comes?"

"Evie Grace, Jesus would be upset if holding up dinner would cause us to miss church. If He comes before we finish, we'll just pass the dish down," said Thomas firmly.

"We can leave a plate on the stove to keep warm for him," added James.

As they finished dinner, Susie started to cut the cake. Evie said, "Susie, the first piece belongs to Jesus. Here's a plate." Susie and Thomas piled mac and cheese on an oven-safe plate in a kettle on very low heat on the gas stove.

The phone rang as they finished. "It's Mom and Dad," called James as he put the phone on speaker. The conversation lasted about twenty minutes. Before the call ended, Kay and Charles sang "We Wish You a Merry Christmas."

Suddenly Kay moaned. Charles said, "We love you. I've got to go."

Thomas came back into the room. "While you guys were talking to your parents, I went outside to check the weather. It's getting worse. I'm sorry to say I don't think we can make it to the church service. We can decorate the tree, sing carols, and read the Christmas story before bed."

"Okey dokey, Grandpa Thomas," replied Evie.

"James Robert, you already plugged in the light strings earlier to test them. Right?" asked Thomas.

"Yes, I'll help you to string the lights and tinsel around the tree," said James Robert.

"Fine," said Thomas.

Susie and Evie gathered all the ornaments. In no time, the tree was adorned with handmade decorations old and new intermingled with heirlooms and shiny store-bought treasures.

As Thomas opened the tree topper box, James said, "I want to check on Mariah one last time."

"All right, but take the big lantern with you and be careful," replied Thomas, turning back to the large five-pointed silver star. Thomas stepped to the ladder, handed Evie the star, and gently lifted the child. She carefully put the star on the tree.

"Is it straight, Susie?"

"Perfect. Come on down."

"Okey dokey, sis."

Thomas helped Evie down. "Susie, do you want to put the lights on?"

"Yeah, Grandpa Thomas." She plugged in the cord, but nothing happened.

"Sorry, girls, there must be a loose wire or bad bulbs. When your brother comes in, we'll have to work on it." Just then, everything went dark.

"What happened, Grandpa Thomas?" Both girls' voices quivered slightly.

"Don't worry, the storm probably knocked out the power. It looks like we'll spend the night camped out by the fireplace to stay warm."

"What fun!" exclaimed Evie Grace.

Just then, James came running in—lantern still in hand. "Thomas, Mariah the mare is in labor."

"Oh my. James, please get the girls' coats and boots. Everyone get ready quickly. We have to get to the barn."

Evie asked, "What about Jesus's dinner?"

"Honey, the electric going off has nothing to do with the gas stove. His meal will stay warm. Now Mariah needs us."

Before opening the door, Thomas took the oil lantern and ordered everyone to hold hands and not let go until they got in the barn. Snow flurries were heavy as they made their way to the barn. The wind was so strong it was all Thomas and James could do to open and then close the barn doors.

Once inside, Thomas added more wood to the barn stove. Thomas said, "Girls, we could be here a while. Why don't you sing Christmas carols softly like a lullaby to keep Mariah calm until the foal comes." Time passed as Evie and Susie gently petted Mariah while they sang. Toward the end of the labor, Evie started to cry.

"Grandpa Thomas, she is really hurting. Can't we do something? Mommy's having a baby. I hope she doesn't hurt like that too. Does she?"

Thomas gave Evie a hug. "Mariah's labor is almost over. After the foal comes, the pain goes away. Your mother is in the hospital. Doctors will make sure she is not hurting. I have to go out and check the weather again. If you need me, just yell."

Thomas swiftly stepped out a side door of the barn. The snow had slowed considerably. As he gazed steadfastly on the sky, he prayed. *Dear Lord, You know from my childhood I asked forgiveness of my sin. You became my savior. My beloved Hattie knew you both as savior and friend. I never really understood that. Lord, you created all things and then died on the cross for people like me. I always felt awkward asking for anything when you have already given me so much. Please help me to draw closer to you and return my joy.*

Little Evie has the same kind of faith and spunk as my Hattie. She is way too young to experience the sadness that has taken my joy. Oh, and, Lord, could you do something with that piece of cake and the birthday supper plate. It would me so much to her and me. Thank you, Amen.

As Thomas turned back to the barn, James Robert screamed, "Grandpa Thomas, something is happening. Hurry!"

Thomas raced inside knelt by Mariah and soon delivered healthy twin foals.

"What will we call them?" asked an excited Evie Grace.

Susie suggested, "Let's call the one…Tidings of Great Joy."

James added, "The other foal is a little stallion with a star on his forehead. How about…Star of Bethlehem."

"Sounds good to me," exclaimed Thomas. As the foals got strong enough to stand, they took their first shaky steps to Mariah to eat. Thomas looked at his watch in the lantern's glow. "Oh my, it's well past midnight. Mariah and her foals are all right now. Let's give them privacy to get to know each other. It's bedtime—we better get back to the house."

"Grandpa Thomas, I wonder if Jesus came?" asked Evie. "Did we miss Santa?"

Susie frowned, "I forgot to leave a piece of cake and glass of milk out for Santa."

"Oh my, we have to fix that—let's hurry. Maybe Santa didn't come yet," scolded Evie.

"Don't worry, sis," stated James, "we'll get 'er done."

"Okay, kids, let's get going.'

As Thomas reached the porch door, he unlocked the door and ushered the kids in quickly to keep the cold out. To his surprise, the electricity was back on and the entire house was toasty warm.

"Look, Grandpa Thomas, the tree lights are on," said the girls with awe.

I wonder who fixed the tree lights? thought Thomas. James headed to the kitchen to fix Santa's goodies.

James shouted, "Come quick—the dinner is missing!"

Thomas and the girls ran into the kitchen. Thomas gazed at the empty pan that just hours before warmed the plate filled with macaroni and cheese. The stove was turned off.

James opened the frig door and said, "I had put two glasses of milk in here...one for Jesus and one for Santa. There is only one glass in here."

Thomas checked the back door. "It's still locked."

"Grandpa Thomas, why are you so surprised?" asked Susie.

"He came—Jesus came," shouted Evelyn Grace, jumping up and down with excitement. "Look at the table." All the other dishes were cleared, washed, and put away.

The only dishes left on the table were at the table setting in front of the special chair at the head of the table. An empty dinner plate with a trace of cheese, empty milk glass, and an empty dessert plate were stacked neatly by a folded napkin and silverware. A top the dessert plate was a single spent birthday candle.

"I told you he would come!" Evie almost sang with happiness.

"I guess you were right after all," replied Thomas, scratching his head. "Well, James, it's really late. Finish placing Santa's goodies. Then, kids, get ready for bed. We can talk about this tomorrow."

Thomas waited until the children were asleep and then retrieved the gifts and put them under the tree. He was heading for the stairs when he went back to the kitchen. The cake and milk were at the other end of the table. *Well, Santa, I'll eat the goodies you forgot.* He was using a flashlight so he wouldn't wake the kids. While putting the glass back on the table, Thomas's arm bumped the flashlight. It rolled against something. Thomas turned the flashlight on it.

It was a Bible. *I don't remember bringing my Bible downstairs. I would have only done that before leaving for church,* mused Thomas. Suddenly he noticed the name inside the cover. This Bible belongs to Hattie Greling. Thomas nearly dropped the flashlight. He quickly put on one light on to double-check what he saw.

No question, it was Hattie's. *How in the world did Hattie's Bible get here?* After all, he had personally put it on the back of his nightstand ten years ago after Hattie tragically died from injuries caused in a car accident with a drunk driver on icy roads, returning from a Bible study in December. His world changed forever. He felt like he died too and walled out the world including their daughter. Then she moved to Alaska.

As he picked up the Bible, a note fell out. It was Hattie's handwriting. *To my Thomas, I'll always love you. Don't stop living!*

Then he noticed recently marked Bible verses. The first one was Psalm 30:5: "Weeping may endure for a night but joy cometh in the morning." The second was Luke 6:21: "Blessed are you that hunger now for you shall be filled. Blessed are you that weep now for you shall laugh."

Thomas looked toward the ceiling and thanked the Lord for showing him Hattie's last love note to him—a final Christmas gift. He could finally accept his loss. "And, Dear Lord Jesus, thank you for the Bible verses and miracle visit. Happy Birthday, Savior and friend. Thank you for joy and your peace that passes understanding. Merry Christmas." Suddenly, he looked at the kitchen clock—it was nearing 3:00 a.m.

Shortly before seven thirty, Thomas was awakened by the joy and laughter of happy children. Suddenly, he felt like Scrooge coming back to life. He jumped out of bed, dressed, and raced downstairs. He called to the kids to get dressed.

"While we're waiting for the sweet rolls to bake, I'm going to read the Christmas story. Since we missed church due to the storm, let's not forget the reason for the season." The children listened intently and then enjoyed a brunch of sweet rolls and scrambled eggs.

Before the children could start to open gifts, the first of two calls came in. It was Charles. Thomas put it on speaker. "Merry Christmas,

James Robert, Susie Kay, and Evelyn Grace—your mother sends her love too. Thomas told me how you girls asked Jesus into your hearts. That's wonderful! I'll tell Kay. She is resting right now. We are so proud of all of you.

"We had twins! And we will be home in a couple weeks as soon as the doctors clear your brother and sister to travel. Nicholas Charles Johnson and Noel Joy Johnson were born about ten o'clock last night. But the phones were out due to large blizzard."

The children were dancing around the room in sheer joy. Thomas said, "Congratulations, Charles."

"Thank you, Thomas, and I have something else to tell. The equipment and the business I used to do will be going back into operation in Pleasantville."

"That's just five miles from here."

"I can do most of the work over the Internet, so, Thomas, if you want me permanently as a farm hand, just say so.

"You bet I'll say so. Also, you know the cottage is too small for your family. When you guys get back, we'll plan a large addition to it. During the construction, the whole family can stay in my home. Twins can be a handful. I'm sure Joyce can help out."

"Thank you again, Thomas. What a Christmas. It's been one miracle after another."

"You don't know the half of it," said Thomas.

"Well, again, Merry Christmas. Kay and I will call tomorrow," said Charles as the call ended.

The kids finally started to open gifts. The phone rang again, and Thomas was surprised to hear Priscilla's voice on the other end. "Dad, I just felt led to call and wish you Merry Christmas and Happy New Year."

"Honey, I love you and wish there was a way to make it up to you for all the years I emotionally pushed you and your family away."

"Well, you will," replied Priscilla. "My husband William thought after that last big earthquake, it was time to move the family back. He found a job with a new business that's starting at the end of July. Both the job and our farm are within twelve miles of you. We're planning to be home for the fourth of July."

"Wonderful! Praise the Lord. I wish I could send hugs over the phone, but I'll save up of a humdinger of an Independence celebration."

"Dad, you really have changed. Did you meet three spirits last night?"

"No. Just the one and only—I'll explain when I see you in person."

"Well, I've got to go. Love you, Dad. Bye."

Thomas looked out the window. "James, how about you and I do the milking. Hey, girls, you can visit with Mariah, Tidings of Great Joy, and Star of Bethlehem while we finish chores."

"Great! Let's go."

At one, Joyce still had not come. "Kids, there's a lot of snow. Let's build a snow family and fort while waiting." Two o'clock, a massive snow plow came down the lane and stopped in front of the barn. The door opened, and Joyce jumped out. The driver helped her with her packages.

"Is everyone okay? The storm was one of the worst blizzards in decades. I hope the stuff for dinner in the frig is all right. In most places, the power just came on about an hour ago."

Thomas and the kids just looked at each other and shrugged their shoulders. "What are you talking about, Joyce? Our power was off for just a short period of time last night."

"It couldn't be. Electric lines came down all over. A tree came down just before your lane. Not only did it pull down electric lines and phone lines, it totally blocked the lane from the highway. Crews are working on your lines now. Thomas, there's no way you had or have power. That would be impossible."

"Nothing is impossible with God. It's another miracle," said Thomas.

Joyce gasped. "Did the guest of honor show up last night?"

"What do you think? Come on in, we're starving. While you're getting dinner on the table and we're eating, we will tell you all about it."

"Okay, okay," said Joyce as they hurried inside.

Then little Evelyn Grace said, "Grandpa Thomas, you forgot something." She handed him a wrapped gift. Thomas opened it to find a handmade popsicle picture frame adorned with brightly colored buttons. A picture of the children was inside. There were handwritten words on the top and bottom—on top the words "Jesus loves you!" and on the bottom "and so do we!" Thomas smiled and laughed with joy as he walked inside.

10

Just as You Are without One Plea

Most of this novel is not nonfiction, but the problems the characters face are very real—job loss, financial struggles, starting over, family, and health issues. Just like the characters, we can have a lot of problems throughout our lives as well.

Everyone—men, women, adults, teens, the very young, and people who have been around a while all have problems. No one is exempt. Although at times I think we all wish we could be. Problems and bad experiences come in all sizes—minor, major, and everything in between. No matter what the problem or troublesome situation, they all have one common denominator. They usually come unexpectedly and seem on the surface to have no potential for good.

The person can either let the problem control their life or do something about it. To a large extent of how a person deals with problems is their personality.

Do you feel compelled to handle everything by yourself? In essence, you are the master of your own life without thinking about anyone or anything else? What caused this? Maybe you trusted people in the past, which let you down or hurt you, and as a result, it left you with an understandable feeling that you should do everything on your own. I know you may be hurting right now, but that way of thinking is not realistic—it doesn't work in the long run.

You can handle things on your own without owing anyone an explanation of your actions. If you follow this way of thinking through life, I have a question for you. How is life working for you? If you make yourself the master of your life, your world is going to get smaller and smaller as your emotional barricades block more people out. What a lonely life. I feel sorry for you. Not only that but despite what you may think, you will eventually have to answer for your decisions.

To other people in this world and at the end of life, if you have never accepted God's plan of salvation through Jesus His Son, you will have to answer to an angry God. Get off your throne and on your knees to God and His Son before it's too late.

You are probably thinking this writer is crazy. After all, God is love, right? How can a loving God keep someone out of heaven and cast them into hell and eventually the lake of fire?

> The Lord is not slack concerning his promise, as some men count slackness; but is longsuffering to us-ward, not willing that any should perish, but that all should come to repentance. (2 Pet. 3:9)

> For God so loved the world that he gave his only begotten Son, that whosoever believeth in him should not perish, but have everlasting life. (John 3:16)

First, God does not *want* anyone to die in their sin. If the person repents of sin and believes on Jesus, God's Son, he will not perish but have everlasting life. That is a promise of God to His children. But people have a tendency to ignore John 3:17–21.

> For God sent not his Son into the world to condemn the world; but the world through him might be saved.
> He that believeth on him is not condemned: but he that believeth not is condemned already,

because he hath not believed in the name of the only begotten Son of God.

And this is the condemnation, that light is come into the world, and men loved darkness rather than the light, because their deeds were evil.

For every one that doeth evil hateth the light, neither cometh to the light, lest his deeds should be reproved.

But he that doeth truth cometh to the light, that his deeds may be made manifest, that they are wrought in God. (John 3:17–21)

Simply put, if you repent of sin and accept God's gift of Jesus His Son, the light of the world, you will have God's promise of eternal life with him. But if you refuse to repent because you prefer the darkness of this world and living in your sin—instead of Jesus, then of your own freewill, *you will have chosen* God's promise of condemnation to nonrepentant sinners!

God created a place in each of us to dwell. Some people long for something not sure what. They go through life trying to fill that place meant for God with desires for material possessions, relationships, or dark things like drug and alcohol abuse. Then they wonder why their lives are falling apart. God gives everyone freewill. He doesn't want us to act like robots. He wants and longs for our freely given sincere love and worship.

The fear of the Lord is the beginning of knowledge. The fear is not to be afraid of God our Father—but reference—to realize the sheer awe of who He is. The sovereign creator, Father, Son, and Holy Spirit.

Trust in the Lord, and do good: so shall shalt thou dwell in the land, verily thou shalt be fed.

Delight thyself also in the Lord: and he shall give thee the desires of thine heart.

Commit the way unto the Lord: trust also in him; and he shall bring it to pass. (Ps. 37:3–5)

In other words, once you accept salvation, just trust the Lord. He will give you wisdom to know what is right. After he impresses on your heart what is right or good, do it! He will provide for your needs. If you enjoy spending time with the Lord in prayer or reading His word, he will give you the desires of your heart (good desires—nothing that would go against His Holy Word). Commit your lifestyle or whatever good project you are currently working on to God—and he will take things to completion.

Still thinking what's the big deal? God made man a living soul.

> And the Lord God formed man of the dust of the ground, and breathed into his nostrils the breath of life: and man became a living soul. (Gen. 2:7)

Our earthly body dies due to Adam and Eve blowing it in the garden of Eden, but the soul lives on. Our All-Knowing Heavenly Father knew that would happen before it did. Adam and Eve had freewill too, just like us today. They chose not to listen to God's rules. God has ultimate control, and at some point in time—at His choosing, he will put an end to evil. However, until that time, evil people will use freewill as a license to do whatever they want no matter who is hurt or killed!

Don't worry, if you are a Christian, God has a plan. However, if you are a nonrepentant sinner or, worse, yet enjoy or take twisted pleasure in committing evil acts against others, take note God is a God of righteous justice—he will punish to the utmost.

> Fret not thyself because of evildoers, neither be thou envious against the workers of iniquity.
> For they shall soon be cut down like the grass, and wither as the green herb. (Ps. 37:1–2)

> Rest in the Lord, and wait patiently for him: fret not thyself because of him who prospereth in

his way, because of the man who bringeth wicked
devices to pass.

Cease from anger, and forsake wrath: fret
not thyself in any wise to do evil.

For evildoers shall be cut off: but those that
wait upon the Lord, they shall inherit the earth.

For yet a little while, and the wicked *shall
not be:* thou shall diligently consider his place,
and it *shall not be.* (Ps. 37:7–10)

The wicked plotteth against the just, and
gnasheth upon him with his teeth.

The Lord shall laugh at him (the evildoer)
for he see that his day is coming. (Ps. 37:12–13)

But the transgressors shall be destroyed
together: the end of the wicked shall be cut off.
(Ps. 37:38)

God is not saying ignore evil but do not spend time worrying about evildoers. And if on the surface it looks like someone is
prospering for evildoing, do not envy them. They will pay for their
wrongdoing. *Do no evil—God will punish.* As I mentioned above,
God is all-knowing, and His plan of salvation was from the very
beginning.

Forasmuch as ye know that ye were not
redeemed with corruptible things, as silver or
gold, from your vain conversation received by
tradition from your fathers:

But with the precious blood of Christ, as of
a lamb without blemish and without spot:

Who verily *was foreordained before the foundation of the world,* but was manifest in these last
times for you. (1 Pet. 18–20; emphasis added)

75

The point is, you cannot buy or earn your salvation. Christ, the Son of God, who knew no sin, took our sin and shed His blood and gave His life for us. To provide the only way back to God. It was planned before time began. Praise the Lord!

The big deal when our physical body dies is we will either. As a Christian, be present with the Lord or as a nonbeliever outer darkness—*the decision is yours.*

By now, you are doing some serious thinking or screaming, *How I could be so intolerant of someone else's beliefs?* I think that is why some churches or pastors don't explain about the need of salvation or the realness of hell. I wonder how many people who turn their backs on God and find themselves in torment will scream political correctness ultimately put them there, all because loving Christians were either afraid of being labeled an intolerant hater or afraid of hurting someone's feelings.

These people's own decision against God put them there, but let us not forget Christians are called to be disciples. There are interesting verses in Ezekiel. Chapter 33 speaks about having a watchman on duty to alert people to danger and blow a trumpet (or shofar) when danger is present. When people hear the trumpet and prepare—great! *If the watchman sounds a warning of danger and some people ignore the warning and dies, he has brought it on himself, but the watchman is in the clear because he did his job and warned the people.* It's not the watchman's fault that some did not listen to him—he tried to tell them but they would not hear him. *If, however, there is danger or a time of trouble and the watchman does not warn that* peoples' lives are in danger and people die, they die in their *own iniquity or sin! But the watchman is in trouble because he did not do his job!*

> When I say unto the wicked, O wicked *man,* thou shalt surely die; if thou dost not speak to warn the wicked from his way, that wicked *man* shall die in his iniquity; but his blood will I require at thine hand. Nevertheless, if thou warn the wicked of his way to turn from it; if he do not turn from his way, he shall die in his iniquity;

but thou hast delivered thy soul. (Ezek. 33:8–9;
emphasis added)

As Christians, we are called to love others—Christian and
non-Christian alike. In caring gentle love, I would rather risk hurting your feelings—now in the short term—rather than you spending
eternity in torment. *I guarantee your feelings won't mean anything then!*

Did you ever watch the news and see different forest fires raging
out of control? Eventually courageous firefighters working hard stop
them. But flames of hell and the lake of fire will not be quenched. In
the Bible when God repeats himself, he's not forgetful—far from it.
He is trying to make a point—to get through our thick skulls. Like
when the resurrected Christ told Peter three times, "Feed my sheep
and lambs." When I hunted up in Strong's Concordance about fire
and the worm, I was surprised tonight to see something I had not
seen before.

In the book of Mark, Jesus repeats something word for word,
not just once or twice but *three times. My personal opinion, he is drawing attention to the fact that hell and never-ending punishment is as real
as you or I. You and I are real; this world is real. Just like God through
Jesus created this world, people, and everything, please don't doubt that
He created hell and the lake of eternal fire as a place of permanent punishment for the devil, fallen angels, and any person whose name is not
written in the Book of Life.*

Where their worm dieth not, and the fire is
not quenched. (Mark 9:44, 46, 48)

Do you really want to risk being there? Hell is no joke. There's
no fire insurance or air conditioners there. There's no toasting marshmallows—*you will be the toast!* There is no undo button or a do-over.
You have your entire life—however long or short—to decide and no
more!

That's why God sent His son Jesus and gave us the Bible so
we can know him. It's the Owners Manuel for *life*. BIBLE—*Basic
Instruction Before Leaving Earth*. If you have a Bible, blow the dust

off it and read it. It does you no good unless you read it. If you have trouble understanding the words, pray and ask for wisdom. And find a Bible-believing church.

Are you still so stubborn that you still doubt if God will cast someone into outer darkness? How about an earthly example? Let's assume you know someone who needs help. Just as we need God's help and he offers it through His Son Jesus. You offer earthly help to the one in need. The person wants to live forever in your home, but before they move in, you find out the person hates you, lies, and steals among other things. In addition, they blatantly state they will not honor your household rules and will do whatever they please or want without regard to your wishes. In essence, thumbing their nose at you. Would you *still* want them to live in your home? Of course not! *So what makes you think the God of the universe—the Great I Am—would allow a nonrepentant sinner in heaven either?*

Think about it! I don't know who is reading this, but before moving on to the next chapter, I pray the Lord uses this to reach the unsaved. Please confess your sin and accept Jesus for Savior. If you have Jesus, praise the Lord. Brother or sister in Christ, someday I look forward to meeting you in heaven.

11

Which Character Are You?
Let Your Light Shine!

Christians have problems too, but there is one big difference. When a Christian encounters problems, they don't have to go it alone. All they need to do is call on the Lord in prayer, and He is there to give heavenly wisdom and strength to go through the situation and overcome as victor.

> Now unto him that is able to exceeding abundantly above all that we ask or think, according to the power that worketh in us, Unto him be glory in the church by Christ Jesus throughout all ages, world without end. Amen. (Eph. 3:20–21)

In other words, use your faith in Him and watch God work!

In the previous chapter, we were talking about personalities. I've already spent a lot of time on one personality—the person who puts himself on the throne of his life, for whatever reason—instead of God! How sad? If the person doesn't ask God to change them, they are banishing themselves from the Lord.

Of the different characters in this book, which are you?

Charles: A hardworking Christian who thought his life was all figured out. The rug was pulled out underneath him. Fears started to arise. He had to relearn to rely on the Lord.

> And be ye not conformed to with world: but be ye transformed by the renewing of your mind, that ye may prove what is that good and acceptable, and perfect will of God. (Rom. 12:2)

> For all things are for your sakes, that the abundant grace might through the thanksgiving of many redound to the glory of God. For which cause we faint not; but though our outward man perish, yet the inward *man* is renewed day by day. (2 Cor. 4:15–16)

Don't let the things and problems of the world pull you down. Don't accept things on the world's terms. Look at the world and problems from God's point of view. Be renewed daily through God's word, prayer, and God's abundant grace.

Kay: A person of strong faith who holds on to the promises of God.

James: A teen who rightly or wrongly feels like they are carrying the worries of the whole world on his shoulders. You don't have to be a teen to feel this way. Just call on Jesus. Only He can give the peace that passes understanding.

> God is our refuge and strength, a very present help in trouble. (Ps. 46:1)

> Be still, and know that I *am* God: I will be exalted among the heathen; I will be exalted in the earth. (Ps. 46:10)

> *Thou wilt keep him* in perfect peace, *whose* mind is stayed *on thee:* because he trusted in thee. (Isa. 26:3; emphasis added)

Susie and *Evelyn Grace*: The sweet, trusting innocence of childhood. The important points: they were not afraid to ask Thomas questions about God, Jesus, sin, and salvation that they did not understand. Once they understood, they asked Jesus into their lives.

If you are a child or adult and have not accepted Jesus because there are things you don't understand, ask a believer in Christ. Don't be ashamed to ask—your soul is on the line.

And if you are a child or adult believer, be prepared to take time to answer those questions in a loving way. Pray with the people asking the questions and for them. Ask God to give them strength and wisdom. Invite the people to church or Bible study. Don't forget that just as God has sent and continues to send people into your life to help you along life's way, be a mentor and ask God how you can help others.

> Dear Lord,
> I pray whoever reads this and has questions—that you send people into their lives that provide the answers. Also provide the people with questions with the boldness and bravery of a child to ask. Thank you, Jesus. Amen.

Point 2: These two sisters had childlike faith—no doubt—for miracles. No matter what our age, we all need to rely on God to get the job done—no matter how impossible the problem may be.

> Jesus answered and said unto them, Verily I say unto you, If you have faith, and doubt not, ye shall not only do this *which is done* to the fig tree, but also if ye shall say unto this mountain, Be thou removed, and cast into the sea; it shall be done.
> And all things, whatsoever ye shall ask in prayer, believing, ye shall receive. (Matt. 21:21–22; emphasis added)

Thomas: A Christian who was stuck in a season of grief. Anyone can get stuck in a problem. Sometimes instead of asking for God's strength to get us through, we can fall into the trap of trying to handle things in our own strength. Then we get in a rut, and before you know, the rut widens and deepens into a pit. Then if we still continue on our own, the pit will get deeper and deeper until the Lord's hand reaches down and lifts us out.

> I waited patiently for the Lord; and he inclined unto me, and heard my cry.
>
> He brought me up also out of an horrible pit, out of the miry clay, and set my feet upon a rock, *and* established my goings.
>
> And he hath put a new song in my mouth, *even* praise unto our God: many shall *see it*, and fear, and shall trust in the Lord.
>
> Blessed *is* that man that maketh the Lord his trust, and respecteth not the proud, nor such as turn aside *to lies*.
>
> Many, O Lord my God, *are* thy wonderful works *which* thou hast done, and thy thoughts *which are* to us-ward: they cannot be reckoned up in order unto thee: *if* I would declare and speak *of them*, they are more than can be numbered. (Ps. 40:1–5; emphasis added)

In plain English, I personally feel if we wait on the Lord, He will hear our prayer for help. Rescue us from our pit (or problem) and set our feet upon a rock. *I wonder if by mentioning a single rock here if God means we need to stand on the Rock of Christ His Son as the foundation of our lives and the path God wants for us will happen.* We will be so happy with what God and Jesus have done that we will be singing *praises to Him* and others will see what God has done. They will have reverence to Him and come to trust Him too. Blessed is the person who trusts in the Lord—don't trust in lies or people who think they know it all. God has done so many wonderful things already, *and we cannot imagine what God has planned for us.* God and Jesus have done so much; their acts cannot be numbered.

While you are in the pit, start praising the Lord! Pray to God and release the situation to him. Let Him handle it as *only He can!*

One very important thing I must mention in regard to lies. There are a number of God-fearing, Bible-believing churches that rightly believe that Jesus is the only begotten Son of God:

1. Was born of a virgin
2. Born in Bethlehem (came in the flesh)
3. Went to the cross and shed his blood for our salvation and healing
4. In three days rose again as the first fruits of eternal life
5. He's coming back for his bride—the church (believers *in Him—Gentiles and Messianic Jews together*)

There are some people and so-called churches that deny some or all of the above five points. When we become Christians, Jesus sends the Comforter, the Holy Spirit, to us. One caution, not all spirits are of God.

> Beloved, believe not every spirit, but try the spirits whether they are of God: because many false prophets are gone out into the world. Hereby know ye the Spirit of God: Every spirit that confesseth that Jesus Christ is come in the flesh is of God: And every spirit that confesseth not that Jesus Christ is come in the flesh is not of God: and this is that *spirit* of the antichrist, whereof ye have heard that it should come: and even now already is it in the world. Ye are of God, little children, and have overcome them: because greater is he that is in you, than he that is in the world.
>
> They are of the world: therefore speak they of the world, and the world heareth them. We are

of God: he that knoweth God heareth us; he that
is not of God heareth not us. Hereby know we
the spirit of truth, and the spirit of error. (1 John
4:1–6; emphasis added)

If a spirit comes to you, ask it if Jesus came to earth? If it says
yes, great, it's from God! If not, don't listen to it. It's from the devil.
The children of God have overcome the devil and the world because
greater is Jesus that is in you than the devil that is in the world.

Joyce: A Christian who enjoys helping people and is open to
miracles.

For by grace are you saved though faith; and
not of yourselves: *it is* the gift of God:
Not of works, lest any man should boast.
For we are his workmanship, created in Christ
Jesus unto good works, which God hath before
ordained that we should walk in them. (Eph.
2:8–10; emphasis added)

For as the body without the spirit is dead,
so faith without works is dead also. (James 2:26)

By faith in God's gift of grace through His Son Jesus is the only
way back to God. However, once you are saved, you will have desire
to do good works. The works or good actions do not save, but the
actions are a result of what God has already done in you. An outward
way to show people and the world your faith in God. If you don't
want to show that faith, you have a problem.

You may be thinking I do not have a lot of money to give. You
can give of your time. Help in nursery at church. Take a dinner to
someone ill. Give someone a ride to church or volunteer at a charity.
If you are homebound, you can pray for others—love for others tran-
scends distance, time, and other limitations.

Engineer: There are a lot of good engineers. Please understand
I'm not saying anything against engineers. I'm simply using this as an

example of a type of personality. He cares about his passengers but puts so much emphasis on his schedule that he was willing to risk the safety of others.

Doing things right on the job is important. However, if you have the same personality as the engineer at the beginning, you have a problem. No one is perfect. The only perfect person to walk this earth was and is—now through us—Jesus. We do need to plan up to a point so we don't go aimlessly through life and have nothing of lasting value at the end.

If, however, you are run by your schedule instead of you controlling the schedule, then there may be times when others are put at risk to their needs or safety being ignored. Later, the engineer realized his error and asked for forgiveness. If your schedule is so controlling that you have no time for others or yourself, ask the Lord for his help before you burn out.

Meteorologist: A voice from the sea of people in life willing to speak up about what is right, especially when so many in the world are willing to be misled to follow the crowd in wrongdoing. We don't know the day and hour of Jesus return, but as time gets closer, more people will be drawn to him. However, some people will go the other way. And in doing so, their thinking will be turned upside—perverted; wrong will be right and right will be wrong.

> But the path of the just *is* as a shining light,
> that shineth more and more to that perfect day.
> The way of the wicked *is* darkness they
> know not at what they stumble.
> *The perfect day refers to the Lord's return.*
> (Prov. 4:18–19; emphasis added)

Now and in the future, God wants His children to speak up for Him and what is right. As more people speak in unity and the righteousness of God—praise the Lord—the stronger the voice.

However, even better, don't hide in the sea of humanity; walk forward, and in addition to united voice, let God's light within you shine as beacon to all those around you. The more people who realize this, the better it will be. This world needs a revival—another awakening.

Dear Lord, let it be. Thank you for those you will call. Amen.

Usually most people hate to hear the alarm clock go off in the morning and hit the snooze button; oh, for a while longer and roll back over. Some just want to ignore the time and what's going on around them. At some point in time—and only God the Father knows when—the alarm clock of time will resound for God's final countdown to setting things straight. Man cannot reset God's plan. Jesus the morning star is coming.

> I Jesus have sent mine angel to testify unto you these things in the churches. I am the root and the offspring of David, *and* the bright and morning star. (Rev. 22:16; emphasis added)

This is just a single verse from the last chapter in the Bible, but please remember this whole book is just as important to read as the rest of the Bible! It is well worth reading—even though parts may be hard to understand—it's Jesus way of letting us know what he wants us to know about what is to come. Read the whole Bible—as you read it, ask for understanding and God will impress on you what he wants to show you.

Do you know people who have not accepted Jesus as Savior and Lord? You don't have to be a missionary to some distant foreign land to preach the Gospel. God may call some disciples to go over the world; however, bloom where you are planted. No matter what your age or gender, you can and must reach people for God. *If Christians don't, who will?*

God gave us different talents, not only for our use but primarily for His use to bring people into the kingdom. The twenty-fifth chapter of Matthew speaks at length about this.

> His lord said unto him, Well done, *thou* good and faithful servant: thou hast been faithful over a few things, I will make thee ruler over

many things: enter thou into the joy of thy lord. (Matt. 25: 21, 23; emphasis added)

Then...

Then he which had received the one talent came and said, Lord, I knew thee that thou art an hard man, reaping where thou hast not sown, and gathering where thou hast not sown, and gathering where thou hast not strawed:

And I was afraid, and went and hid thy talent in the earth: lo, *there* thou hast *that is* thine.

His lord answered and said unto him, *Thou* wicked and slothful servant, thou knewest that I reap where I sowed not, and gather where I have not strawed:

Thou oughtest therefore to have put my money to the exchangers, and *then* at my coming I should have received mine own with usury.

Take therefore the talent from him, and give *it* unto him which have ten talents.

For unto every one that hath shall be given, and he shall have abundance: but from him that hath not shall be taken away even that which he hath.

And cast ye the unprofitable servant into outer darkness; there shall be weeping and gnashing of teeth. (Matt. 25:24–30; emphasis added)

You really should read the entire chapter—Jesus really spells it out. Concerning the last days and explaining the difference between good and bad servants in depth. I personally feel that the word *talents* can have more than one meaning. First, obviously, money, but it can mean talents to do things or using your possessions wisely. Remember, all that we have come from God to begin with. We came into this world owning nothing, and we cannot take any physical possessions with us. As I said before, no one is perfect—me included. We at times may regret missed opportunities for God. Thank goodness He is forgiving. But if people know of God, religion, but don't know him, relationship, they will not use the things God gave them in the way God intended. Look out! When these people hide talents, money, and possessions and don't use them at all to increase reaching people for the Lord, the Lord will cast them into outer darkness! *I pray to Jesus that anyone that reads this does not end up in outer darkness!*

One word of caution when trying to reach people for Christ, don't do this in your own strength and end up forcing your beliefs down people's throats. If you do this, no matter how well meaning to save souls, all you will end up doing is drive people in the devil's direction.

Before you witness to someone, pray about it *first.* Listen to what God lays on your heart about it because he also knows what's on that person's heart and mind as well. If you are still unsure about how to witness in Christian love and don't want to blow it, ask your pastor or church.

See if they have any witnessing teams or discipleship classes. If they do, great. If they don't, you may feel led by God to find another church that believes the Bible is the unerring word of God and reaches out to help others—both Christian and non-Christian. Or God may lay it on your heart to start such a ministry in your church or community that does not have one.

Dear Lord, if someone is considering this in the name of Jesus, I pray you give them the wisdom to do this and give them the people and resources for the job. Let us never forget you're the one in charge. Shut whatever doors that would hinder and open whatever doors are needed to do your will. Praise your holy name. Thank you for what you are doing and will do. Amen.

Pastor from the Crowd: I let this pastor unnamed since I don't want people to jump to the conclusion I'm pastor or church bashing. There are many God-fearing Christians and ministers. But I feel led to point out there seems to be a spirit of complacency or indifference out there. Maybe some believers could be misunderstanding being separate.

> Be ye not unequally yoked together with unbelievers: for what fellowship hath righteousness with unrighteousness? And what communion hath light with darkness?
>
> And what concord hath Christ with Belial? Or what part hath he that believeth with an infidel?
>
> And what agreement hath the temple of God with idols? For ye are the temple of the living God; as God hath said, I will dwell in them, and walk in *them;* and I will be their God, and they shall be my people.
>
> Wherefore come out from among them, and be ye separate, saith the Lord, and touch not the unclean *thing;* and I will receive you.
>
> And will be a Father unto you, and ye shall be my sons and daughters, saith the Lord Almighty. (2 Cor. 6:14–18; emphasis added)

In other words, living like God wants us to live. Don't have a lifestyle of deliberate sinning like the world. In essence, don't live like the devil. Major point, we are not of the world—just passing through—but *for now, we are in the world.* And because we are in the world we need, in fact, we should reach out to others with God's love and the Gospel.

As a Christian, when we occasionally slip and fall in sin, Jesus is our mediator, but the Holy Spirit within us keeps us from living a sinful lifestyle when we truly know Jesus as savior. Some may think let's just stay in the church and leave the world outside, but they forget what Jesus told the disciples after His resurrection right before he was received up into heaven to sit at the right hand of God.

> Go ye into all the world, and preach the gospel to every creature.

> He that believeth and is baptized shall be
> saved; but he that believeth not shall be damned.
> (Mark 16:15–16)

Also just read in Revelation, Jesus's letters to the churches. He clearly states what they are doing right and emphatically states what they are doing wrong.

So just as the letters represent a named early church for an area, I have heard pastors preach that today each letter represents a different type of church. What each church is doing the good and the bad. The church building or physical structure can be built of wood, brick, stone, etc. But as the Bible states, the body is the temple.

> What? Know ye not that your body is the
> temple of the Holy Ghost *which is* in you, which
> ye have of God, and ye are not own?
> For ye are bought with a price: therefore
> glorify God in your body, and in your spirit,
> which are God's.
> God's spirit lives in us and Jesus bought us
> through his life's blood. (1 Cor. 6:19–20; emphasis added)

I personally wonder if the letters represent types of churches—and we are ourselves are the temple or church of God; for God to dwell, is there a double meaning? First, the corporate church body as a whole, comprised of many member churches. Secondly, we as individual temples of God are accountable to God for good and bad alike.

Now at this point, please don't misunderstand what I'm trying to say. If you sincerely accepted Jesus as savior, He is indeed our mediator when we screw up. And there are times when I myself feel like a giant screw up. When we mess up, just call on Jesus and ask for forgiveness.

> For *there is* one God, and one mediator
> between God and men, the man Christ Jesus. (1
> Tim. 2:5; emphasis added)

God will not zap from above, but we can grieve the Holy Spirit.

> And grieve not the holy Spirit of God, whereby ye are sealed unto the day of redemption.
> Let all bitterness, and wrath, and anger, and clamour, and evil speaking, be put away from you, with all malice:
> And be ye kind one to another, tenderhearted, forgiving one another, even as God for Christ's sake hath forgiven you. (Eph. 4:30–32)

But when you get a chance to reach out to others please do it.

> The harvest truly *is* plenteous, but the labourers *are* few;
> Pray ye therefore the Lord of the harvest, that he will send forth labourers into his harvest. (Matt. 9:37–38; emphasis added)

Some churches or denominations conduct church business, ministries, or church services with such structured procedures or adhere to a strict order of things it leads to problems. Structure or orderly planning is fine up to a point. Without any biblical structure or planning, there would be chaos or irreverence to God. But if people get so caught up *strictly* in the customs or process of running the church *alone*, whether inadvertently or deliberately, we are in *big* trouble. That would be no better than how some scribes and Pharisees, Jesus warned the people about, handled things.

When that happens, the church is teaching religion—*and not the importance* of every person needing to have a *personal relationship* with *Jesus*.

If a church is having difficulty drawing the unsaved in, it might be more than the people feeling awkward over guilt of their sin. The problem could be they see the religion of the church and either miss or misunderstand the all-important message of relationship.

Or the church is afraid to preach the fire and brimstone of God's Holy Word because of political correctness or hurting feelings. Or worse yet, think they have to always make people feel good and entertain them.

> I charge thee therefore before God, and the Lord Jesus Christ, who shall judge the quick and the dead at his appearing and his kingdom;
> Preach the word; be instant in season, out of season; reprove, rebuke, exhort with all longsuffering and doctrine.
> For the time will come when they will not endure sound doctrine; but after their own lusts shall they heap to themselves teachers, having itching ears;
> And they shall turn away *their* ears from the truth, and shall be turned unto fables.
> But watch thou in all things, endure afflictions, do the work of an evangelist, make full proof of thy ministry. (2 Tim. 4:1–5; emphasis added)

The congregation (audience) may never realize the true cost of the entertainment is their souls until the end of this life. When they wake up to front-row seats in hell, no entertainment then—just suffering. How horrible what a loss!

They validly earned the right to be there because they did not make a decision for Jesus and God. There is no fence sitting for Jesus.

> He that is not with me is against me: and he that gathereth not with me scattereth. (Matt. 12:30 and Luke 11:23)

If you did not say no to Jesus's gift, it still has the same result as not saying yes to Jesus Savior and Lord.

However, when we see the Lord face-to-face—and we all will someday—and they're handing out various crowns, what will you ask Him? How might the conversation go? What will you answer him if He asks you questions? Child, I love you, but I loved you and everyone else so much that I gave my life instead of you and others to save mankind. No one could save themselves—only I can save. Each person has to live throughout eternity with their decision or lack of decision. Why didn't you love me enough to take time to tell the unsaved about me? And also tell them about my Father God's love and mine and the sealing power of the Holy Spirit?

> That if thou shalt confess with thy mouth the Lord Jesus, and shalt believe in thine heart that God hath raised him from the dead, thou shalt be saved.
>
> For with the heart man believeth unto righteousness; and with the mouth confession is made unto salvation.
>
> For the scripture saith, Whoever believeth on him shall not be ashamed.
>
> For there is no difference between the Jew and the Greek: for the same Lord over all is rich unto all that call on him.
>
> For whosoever shall call upon the name of the Lord shall be saved.
>
> How then shall they call on him in whom they have not believed? And how shall they believe in him of whom they have not heard? And how shall they hear without a preacher?
>
> And how shall they preach, except they be sent? As it is written, How beautiful are the feet of them that preach the gospel of peace, and bring glad tidings of good things!
>
> But they have not all obeyed the gospel. For Esais saith, Lord who hath believed our report?

So then faith *cometh* by hearing, and hearing by the word of God. (Rom. 10:9–17; emphasis added)

I know there appears to be more info in this section than is needed but not really. Four of the first five verses refer to people praying the prayer of salvation. *The fourth verse sheds light on a major issue.* When the apostle Paul was saying there is no difference between the Jew and the Greek, he meant no difference between Jew and Gentile. After Jesus was crucified years later, misguided people started what is called replacement theology. *They thought and taught* that Jews lost their standing as the apple of God's eye, thinking that they had killed Jesus and were replaced by the church. *How wrong!*

I say then, Hath God cast away his people? God forbid. For I also am an Israelite, *of* the tribe of Benjamin.

God hath not cast away his people which he foreknew. Wot ye not what the scripture saith Elias? how he maketh intercession to God against Israel saying,

Lord they have killed thy prophets, and digged down thine alters; and I am left alone, and they seek my life.

But what saith the answer of God unto him? I have reserved to myself seven thousand men, who have not bowed the knee to *the image of* Baal.

Even so then at this present time also there is a remnant according to the election of grace. (Rom. 11:1–5; emphasis added)

Major point: the reason!

I say then, Have they stumbled that they should fall? God forbid: but *rather* through their fall salvation *is come* unto the Gentiles, for to provoke them to jealousy. (Rom. 11:11; emphasis added)

Now let's get back to what Romans 14–17 really means. People have to hear about God and Jesus before they can believe. There needs to be people to go preach to people.

Christian, please consider about what your conversation with Jesus would be like. Would there be things you wish you could still change? Well, if you are reading this, remember, you are still on this side of heaven. Don't you want to do something *now*? *Now only* *w*hile there's time!

When we are in heaven, we will enter into our rest. A time of great joy, no more pain, wiping away of tears. As a physically challenged women—wholeness. Just think in the figurative sense (May the Lord and the reader grant me a little poetic license due to the extreme joy I'm experiencing now just thinking about then).

All wheelchairs, walkers, crutches, canes, braces, prosthetics, glasses, dentures—whatever you and I have now that we wish we didn't. They will be checked and tossed away before entering the pearly gates. Never to be needed again.

We will have new bodies. Not only that we will be reunited with deceased loved ones that made the same decision for Christ. Never to be separated from our family again. It's beyond words what it will be like and how we will feel. Jesus talked about doing His Father's work while He was on earth and a time when no one could work.

I must work the works of him that sent me,
while it is day: the night cometh, when no man
can work. (John 9:4)

However big point, time is up for witnessing. So reach people in this life while you can.

One thing I feel I must say before finishing the ending story of this character. There is a segment hiding in the shadows that affect saved and unsaved as well. People who think they are Christians and are not. There are two groups. One going through the motions of church and what they perceive is Christianity. The problem is, a legalistic church, minister, or people taught this person religion instead of relationship.

If you are reading this and feel led by the Lord to question if your sincere acceptance of Jesus occurred, you may feel detached like the unnamed pastor. The Holy Spirit may be moving on your heart to change that. If you do feel like you might fall into this category, praise the Lord there is hope for you yet. Just call on him.

If you were christened or sprinkled on as an infant or have saved family and you have the misconception that christening saved you or you inherited salvation from saved family members, that's wrong. That is not biblically correct.

If a baby or young child passes away before being able to know right from wrong, they go to heaven.

> And they brought young children to him, that he should touch them:
> And *his* disciples rebuked those that brought *them*.
> But when Jesus saw *it*, he was much displeased, and said unto them, Suffer the little children to come unto me, and forbid them not: for of such is the kingdom of God. (Mark 10:13–14; emphasis added)

But if you were sprinkled or baptized before you prayed the prayer of salvation, it does not count. Baptism is an outward way of showing of what God's saving grace has already done on the inside. And if you have saved family, that is wonderful, but just because they are saved does not mean you are saved. When Peter went to Cornelius and the family was saved, the Holy Spirit came upon them.

> While Peter yet spake these words the Holy Ghost fell on all which heard the word. (Acts 10:44)

Faith comes by hearing and hearing the Word of God. They heard the Word and accepted Jesus and then the Holy Spirit came. Then they were baptized.

If you have never asked Jesus to forgive your sin, then ask Him into your life right now. If you had previously prayed the pray of salvation but wasn't sincere or did not understand it, pray it now.

If you did have basic understanding and sincerity of heart when you originally prayed the prayer of salvation but feel that your life has veered away, just tell the Lord that you want to recommit your life to Him. Ask Jesus for godly wisdom on what His will is for your life.

God, His Son Jesus and the Holy Spirit are greater than the devil and the fallen angels. Read the end of the Bible—God wins! But until that time, we as Christians have to realize Jesus has already won the war against the devil on the cross but the devil and his workers are trying to blind many people to God's love and plan of salvation. *We cannot let that happen.*

They are ravenous wolves in sheep's clothing. They portray a godly facade. They deliberately mislead unsaved or recently saved (babes in Christ) who have yet to build a strong spiritual foundation that would assuredly expose these dark forces to the light of God.

These people will never accept the salvation of the Lord and sadly deny the power of God. Stay away from people like this. They will only lead you astray and toward destruction. These wolves in sheep's clothing work to try to divide churches or, worse yet, plant seeds of doubt about the Bible causing a falling away from Jesus—the very one that willingly and lovingly gave up *His perfect life* on the cross. "Now the Spirit speaketh expressly that in latter times some shall depart from the faith giving heed to seducing spirits" (1 Tim. 4:1). One of these lies—they are telling people Jesus is not coming back. Truth there is a rapture and a second coming! In the book of John, Jesus speaks about going to prepare a place and then coming to take believers.

How could anyone doubt His return? But one day, in the eighties during a college lunch break with two classmates, I got the shock of my life. The first classmate was a woman in her fifties and the second a young woman in her early twenties if that. All three of us were

Christians. The younger woman excitedly shared how she came to Christ after giving up witchcraft. During the course of the conversation, the topic of the Lord's return came up. The young woman had a question about it. I thought I would let the older woman answer her since by age the woman would be (or should have been) more biblically versed in the answer.

To my surprise, she expressed doubts about Jesus's return. Her reasoning—things were so bad (at that time), why hadn't He come already? Whether she still feels this way, I don't know, but the sadness and deflated look in the young woman's eyes was undeniable. At the time, I did not know about 2 Peter 3:9: "The Lord is not slack concerning his promise, as some men count slackness: but is longsuffering to us-ward, not willing that any should perish but that all should come to repentance."

I immediately spoke up and said, yes, things are bad but things are not as bad as what God thinks is bad enough for the time of His return. The older woman said I might be right. The shocker—the middle-aged woman was a *pastor's wife*.

Again, the time is only known to God the Father. But he has given us a glimpse or foreshadowing of things to come through hidden insights or layers of parables, feasts of the Lord, and ceremonies. Proof of the rapture is the Galilean wedding ceremony. Just watch the detail in the documentary "Before the Wrath," narrated by actor Kevin Sorbo. The documentary is outstanding.

> This know also that in the last days perilous times shall come.
>
> For men shall be lovers of their own selves, covetous, boasters, proud, blasphemers, disobedient to parents, unthankful, unholy.
>
> Without natural affection, trucebreakers, false accusers, in continent, fierce, despisers of those that are good.
>
> Traitors, heady, highminded, lovers of pleasures more than lovers of God;

> Having a form of godliness but denying the
> power thereof: from such turn away. (2 Tim. 3:1–5)

If anyone doubts the relevance of the Bible or the all-knowing power of Almighty God throughout the past, present, near future, and beyond, just take another look at the five scriptures above. Don't just read them. Study them.

It certainly describes the world today to a T. Watch the newscasts or read the paper. The news is chalk full of bad stories or crimes committed by people controlled by the traits listed above.

One part of God's character is all-knowing simply because He is God. And I believe a loving God wants His children to know this stuff ahead of time for at least two reasons. First, to reaffirm or ensure to everyone; only God can know everything thousands of years before it happens—and He is the Great I Am. And second, he wanted them to be prepared and not be sidetracked by the world. He wants us—with his help—to stay on the narrow road of life to Him instead of the wide road or roads—of the world—littered with the snares and banana peels of life just waiting to trip people up.

Finally, the pastor on the train experienced the miracle power of God. He was saved but did not have a personal relationship with God. The storm during the train ride got his attention. *Could God be trying to get your attention through storms in your life?* He learned with every fiber of his being that God, Jesus, and the Holy Spirit are very real and all-powerful. The minister's head knowledge was now heart knowledge. The experience gave him a renewed sense of purpose in life.

If you are like the unnamed pastor, I pray that you ask the Lord to help you become an evangelist. *Time is running out to reach people.* May God bless people with a spirit and heart of great preachers, like Billy Graham and Billy Sunday and other straightforward, plain-talking, caring, God-led preachers. May they lead the way for revival.

Dear Lord, in your Son Jesus's name I ask that you draw these people to you and open up the flood gates of revival around the world. That people will be riding such a big wave of salvation the world will be in awe—all will know *that only God could do this!* May everyone sing your praises. Amen.

12

My Testimony

About the hardest thing about a testimony is getting started. Just say a prayer, take a deep breath, and start. Before you know it, any nervousness will go and you will be testifying of God's goodness along with helping others. Not to mention, you'll feel pretty good yourself because you are doing the will of your father.

And with that being said, I better do myself what I've been telling everybody else to do.

Dear Lord, let my testimony—and this book—do your will. Thank you. Amen.

You cannot hear it, but I'm taking a very deep breath…Here goes…

I'm not saying I'm super special or better than anybody else; I'm not—I'm just like anyone else. The only thing that makes each one of us special is God's love, saving grace, and the talents he has given us. When I was a teenager after a Saturday afternoon Bible study at a friend's home, I suddenly realized I never remembered saying the prayer of salvation. Although I never wrote down the date, I spoke the prayer. Some people remember the exact date, like a second birthday, and there is nothing wrong with that idea. If you remember the date, great, but if you don't know it, don't stress over it either. What's really important is that you did it!

While I was alone—but I wasn't really alone—for a few minutes in my friend's dining room in Windber, Pennsylvania, I prayed the prayer of salvation. But as a child, I always felt close to him. Others have said the same thing too; however, please still pray the prayer of salvation to guarantee relationship with God, Jesus, and the Holy Spirit on God's terms.

I was born in 1964. In a prior book, I already mentioned about my parents adopting me at nine months of age. The disability was there. Little was known except some medical information. I won't bore you with a lot of medical details—but clearly God was in control of the whole thing.

Doctors tried to talk my parents *out of adopting me*. I was born two and a half months ahead of time with cerebral palsy. For the most part back then, babies born that early did not survive. When I was just two weeks old, I had pneumonia. My biological parents called in a priest to christen me before they thought the unenviable happened. I don't know if he also performed last rites or not. If he did, praise the Lord they didn't take.

In the sixties, people cared more for the sanctity of human life than they do now. I pray today that as more people realize that life starts at conception and not at birth, it will mean something again. Also, life is all important at all ages—unborn to a hundred and one plus; love of life will be important again. Remember, Moses was a 120 years old when the Lord called him home!

> And Moses *was* an hundred and twenty years old when he died: his eye was not dim, nor his natural force abated. (Deut. 34:7; emphasis added)

I'm not judging the debate on women's rights, but could a baby that was aborted have found a cure for cancer or other diseases? The ancient nation of Sparta used to abort unwanted babies by abandoning them to the elements. *Sparta is no more.* Roe vs. Wade was in January 1973. Praise the Lord those children are with the Lord. But with my accounting background, I cannot keep from posing a financial question. Some of these babies, if they had lived, would be in their thirties or forties at least. They would have been working and paying into social security. What shape would social security be in with those funds?

God *is in total* control, but the freewill he has given us results in some decisions made by some people being like a game of pickup sticks. Moving just one stick (one decision) starts a chain reaction that affects others. Maybe that seems too simplistic, but think about it.

Now please understand, I'm in no way trying to judge women that had abortions or others involved in abortions. Only God has the right to judge. He is also forgiving. But being disabled with a life, I'm just standing up as a voice for the silent unborn. That is a moving living being inside you! *For God's sake and your sake, don't treat the child or children like a cancerous tumor to be ripped out. The true aggressive cancer is the thinking that encourages and in fact forces the idea that there is nothing wrong at all with the heinous murdering of millions.* In reality, it is a worldwide war against innocents that cannot defend themselves and are unable to ask people to help them.

Someone on the Queue T told my parents that one of my biological parents wanted whatever equipment I was attached to unplugged. Praise the Lord the nurses said no! You didn't even hear the terms *euthanasia* or *assisted suicide* back then. Most love their life as they should; I included.

However, if someone sadly chooses it, people can kill themselves—freewill at work again, but not the way God intended. Two problems with that way of thinking: One, only God has the right to take a life, so even though it is your body, you're playing God. *There is only one God.* And news flash, you or anyone else that thinks this way is not the Almighty. The devil thought that he could be equal to God too, and we all know how that went. Don't kid yourself. The Lord has a final solution for the devil, fallen angels, and anyone that refuses the love and saving grace of God and His Son Jesus. Two, as more people with this wrong thinking push for *their* rights, and no one puts limits on this stuff—before you know it, that same thinking will be used *to force* others *against their freewill* to kill the elderly, disabled, and unwanted in a perverse *so-called* compassion. We also must get medical costs under control, or that same perverse hatred of which some *perceive* to be weak, unwanted, or unable to be productive in society would use *so-called* medical costs savings as a possible reason for *their so-called compassionate murder.*

You think that's crazy. It could not happen in a modern world filled with loving people. It's not the loving people causing the problem. Although I will add, a famous quote from Irish statesman Edmund Burke. Remember, the only thing necessary for the triumph of evil is for good men—*or women*—to do nothing. Let's go back to 1982, the same year I graduated high school. On April fifteenth of that year, a six-day-old baby boy was labeled "Baby Doe" by the court system, and the media died just because he had Down syndrome. He was born with a disconnected esophagus. A doctor advised the parents not to have the surgery. He actually told the parents that there were things worse than a child dying. Living would be worse. How horrid!

Other people came forward to adopt him. The parents said no. For whatever reason, and again, only God can judge, they chose to let their son die rather than let people that were willing and prepared to handle what they were either unable to or did not want to. If you want the in-depth story, read the book *Playing God in the Nursery* by Jeffrey Lyon. Oh, you say, "That's horrible. That could not happen in the twenty-first century." Think again.

Spring of 2018—just search on Google "Alfie Evans." I won't say a lot because his parents have gone through a lot. He was a toddler born with a rare condition. Against his parents' wishes, the hospital in Europe wanted to deny care. When the parents wanted to get care in another nation, they had to fight for their own rights and their son. When the European Court of Human Rights refused to intervene in the case, then many people from around the world stood up for what was right—including the Pope. My big question is, how much stuff could be going on in the world that people don't know about?

This to me is the proof that there is indeed an aggressive cancer of wrong thinking I spoke about above. The tentacles of this hatred-filled cancer are growing and reaching around the world and attempting to take over in cities or communities. The only way to stop it—and there is a way—is for God-fearing Christians to shine the light of God's love on it. To expose this dark thinking to the light so people can start doing what is right and stop the wrongs!

I pray, Lord, that there are people who read this and feel led to reach out to others to help them in a loving way, to do what is right and prevent wrongs that could save lives! As a disabled person, it is very sobering to realize if that wrong thinking was strong when I was born, therefore, but the grace of God go I. Except for God's intervention, I would not be here now!

I'll tell you right now, disability or not, I love the life God has given me. One other thing I'll add. When a murderer is sentenced to death, they were found guilty in court. But even after killing others, they still have the right to appeal for their life and *no one gives that right a second thought.*

Who is going to make the appeal for the life of the innocent unborn before the death sentence of abortion is carried out?

Dear Lord, I pray in a loving way this message reaches someone before they make the life-ending decision of no return. Show them your way of handling their situation and not the world's way. Thank you. Amen.

Please, for the sake of saving yourself from a lifetime of guilt, think about it. In addition, choose life for a child and give them a chance at living just like your parents gave you. If you don't want the abortion but do not want the child either, then choose the other A—adoption. You'll be bringing joy into the lives of others, and there's nothing wrong in that at all.

Before I go on with my testimony, I feel led by the Lord to mention a crazy idea. As I've been writing this, I've been interrupted by two long phone calls and the idea is still there. So I must put it forward. I'm no medical professional and the idea may sound so crazy you may think that she can truly write fiction. I don't even know if it is medically possible. But I still cannot shake the concept that is in my head.

If it works, there would not need to be anymore legal battles over abortion or a woman's right over her body. Just imagine if a woman didn't want a baby, she could go into a hospital or clinic, and have a DNA or blood test done—just like organ donors. The big difference, she would be matched with another woman recorded in a pregnancy bank or registry. To be matched up with a woman who wants the fetus for her own child or would act as a surrogate mother for a woman totally unable to carry a child to term. If someone wants a late-term abortion or if the mother's life is in danger but still wants the child, just build more advanced incubators.

Sounds crazy maybe? But how about it, doctors? Worried about stem cell research or using aborted baby body parts for *humanized mice*? Just use cells harvested from umbilical cords after babies are born. Don't use the cells of a fetus (child). Does using body parts for research mice sound like a Frankenstein horror movie? *It's for real. Just go to CBN news or CNSNews.com and read the story for yourself about the FDA buying aborted baby body parts and tissue.* September 17, 2018—Eighty-five members of Congress signed a letter denouncing the contract. On June 6, 2019, President Trump stopped this, but the next administration in the White House (April 19, 2021) has permitted this baby body parts research. A little bit of medical research for an alternative to abortion could save more lives than take them—novel idea.

Doctors, remember your Hippocratic Oath. Sure, some embryos (babies) might not survive being transplanted from one womb to another and miscarry and die, but the miscarriage rate would be less than 100 percent death rate of abortion. Maybe during the term of the pregnancy, drugs used to prevent transplant rejection could be used provided they would not harm the unborn.

So, doctors, here is my challenge to you. Why don't you try it? Are you afraid to try? Let me speak to your ego—just think of all the accolades you and your colleagues would have if you came up with a viable twenty-first-century solution to the twentieth-century murderous nightmare of ending the lives of unwanted children by abortion. You might even get the Nobel Prize for medicine. Just remember that God gives you the knowledge.

Then future generations would rightly place abortion in history with other wrongs—which at their time in history *seemed okay to some*, like slavery and the Holocaust. According to Google, the total death toll for all US wars are 1,264,000. Let us never forget each number represents a person whose life was cut short due to the unfortunate realities of war. Then, as I researched abortion numbers, I could hardly believe what I was looking at when I found a website called *US Abortionclock.org.* At the time I'm writing this, the total of abortions in the *US since 1973 is over sixty million!* Worldwide abortions since 1980 was *1,580,741,134!* The clock is still running!

Life is sacred. Get real. *Something needs to be done* against *this war on human life. In reality, sacrificing innocents on the altar to the idol of self-absorbed—my body comes first—*must *change.* People *need to wake up* to this deadly wrong thinking that an unborn life is an inconvenience or judge the elderly or disabled as no longer valuable and therefore *according to the world's perverse thinking should do the world a favor and die.* Again, the light of God must expose this darkness. So, Christians, please reach out to the people with the love of God and Jesus His Son and in a loving gentle way show them God's way of doing things before it's too late on God's clock.

President Trump and other prolife politicians and people could encourage doctors to try before any more babies and future constituents are put to death needlessly. Cut through red tape and get things done; if this potentially can be done medically, get 'er done! Please, Mr. Trump, with the Lord's help, get the ball rolling because as you are well aware of the type of heavy opposition that would come against such an idea before research could even start.

If this could be done, not only would it save lives, give childless couples children, and let others go on with their lives, it would bring an end to one contentious rift to this country and around the world. Now that I've said it, I'm glad—I feel this came from God because up until today, I never thought about an answer to abortion.

Now at this point, if you have put this book down, I hope you are doctors prayerfully considering the above solution? Or you may be President Trump seeing how to fund and start the research—you are one of the best at cutting through the red tape of political correctness so wrongs can be righted. I pray the Lord guides and protects you and this country. I also pray the Lord lays this on your heart like mine. Amen.

If you are someone who thinks abortion or ending a baby's life or anyone else's is a good thing, I feel sorry for you. If you would have had your way when I was a baby I would not be living now. If you are this type of person, you have probably thrown this book in the corner, in the garbage, or out the window. If you take a dark satisfaction or a twisted joy in ending lives, just think of this: if you were born after 1973 and you found out your parents were considering abortion, *how would you feel?*

I'm not judging, but you know the saying, put yourself in the other person's shoes. *So put your feet in the unborn babies' booties!* Now that I've handled this controversial subject and possible solution—when I had not planned to do so, I feel it had to be of God. I let Him handle the rest of it.

Now I'll get on with my testimony. As I said, doctors tried to talk my parents out of adopting me. They told them that I would not walk and talk, and I would mentally be a vegetable. They also added that I would not live past my teens. There would be more illness than most kids.

Despite this grim prognosis, my parents were still undeterred. *They knew only God knows the future!* They continued on with the adoption. So just to inform you, if you have not already figured it out, according to the experts, when I was an infant, you are now reading a novel written by a fifty-plus teenage vegetable. *Really?* Praise the Lord!

> But God hath chosen the foolish things of
> the world to confound the wise; and God hath
> chosen the weak things of the world to confound
> the things which are mighty. (1 Cor. 1:27)

My parents took me to Children's Hospital in Pittsburgh. Over my childhood, I had three surgeries—at four, ten, and twelve to walk. The most interesting surgery was when I was ten, I spent a summer in a body cast. What a hot summer, but every few days, God sent a day or two of cooling rain. Then at twelve, I had surgery to lengthen the hamstrings under my knees. It was supposed to be a basic textbook surgery of just an hour or two. The surgery itself went well, but when it came time for me to wake up, there were complications.

That same day, a number of children from the orthopedic ward I was in had various surgeries; some of their surgeries were more involved than mine. As time passed, my parents and the nurses became more and more concerned. Even though for obvious reasons, the operating room frowned on phone calls; my parents told me the nurses made several calls. But they were unable to get any answers. As more hours passed, *all the other kids* were all brought back to the ward to rest, except me.

My parents knew something was very wrong. They told the nurses they were going to the hospital chapel to pray. To this day, I still vividly remember waking up just as though it happened yesterday, but the real story is what God did. When I was older, my mother confided in me what happened that day in the recovery room and the chapel. She also told me about a unique testimony that she and Dad heard several days later.

No other people were there when they got to the chapel. I don't know how long they were praying, but Dad was seated behind Mom and slightly to her right. Suddenly, Mom turned to Dad and asked him, "How do you know she will be all right?" Dad looked surprised. She then questioned him further, "Didn't you just touch my shoulder and tell me *she is all right?*"

Dad answered, "No, and I didn't hear anything."

Mom informed Dad, "Bob, Lorrie is okay. We need to get back upstairs to the ward before she gets back."

They hurried upstairs; they were barely inside the orthopedic ward when the nurse came running to meet them. She had a big smile on her face and told them, "They just called. They're bringing her up. She will be here in a few minutes."

My surgery had started early that morning, and I finally made it back to my bed late that afternoon. My parents and the nurses were grateful, but no one was told at that time what had happened. A day or two later, an anesthesiologist left word that he wanted to talk to my parents. While I was resting and napping normally, they had a conference with him. He explained that after my surgery and

I did not wake up, they discovered I was allergic to one of the drugs they used. He wanted to make sure my parents were told so that if I ever needed any kind of surgery in my lifetime, all my records should include info on the allergy.

He then began to tell them about happened in that recovery room and why they did not tell the nurses anything. *I will add something in here before I go with what he said. Just in case you're not familiar with operating and recovery procedures, after a surgery, people are moved into recovery to closely be monitored by skilled professionals who make sure the patients wake up and have recovered enough to go back to their rooms. Generally, people are not in recovery for a long time.*

The surgery lasted the expected time of a few hours. Nothing seemed wrong until shortly after the gurney I was on was wheeled into the recovery room. The anesthesiologist went on to tell my parents in a serious somber voice what happened next. They thought at first I was just a little slow at waking up. As a little time passed, the doctors realized that was not the case. When the nurses called, the doctors could not tell them when I would be out of recovery because I was still in deep sleep and they were still trying different ways to get me awake. A whole group of doctors at this point was working on me. Things that worked to wake others did not work.

Then the doctors, in a decision of last resort, pulled out a defibrillator—the same equipment that can be used when someone has a heart attack. *Nothing was or is wrong with my heart.* But drastic problems call for drastic measures. He added they didn't know what else to try.

Their last hope to save my life was shocking my body with the electric charge from the defibrillator. *It did not work*—I remained in deep sleep. As the seriousness of the situation began to sink in, the anesthesiologist said everyone was standing and looking around at each other wondering who was going to tell my parents—the surgery was a success, but their daughter who was only twelve years old, their only child, would never wake up.

Then suddenly it was if a light turned on. Your daughter woke up. Within a very short time, she was even talking to us—knew where she was and fully alert. Everyone was joyous but could not understand what had happened. She woke up only after the doctors had given up working on her.

My parents asked him if he was a Christian. He said yes, but he admitted he wasn't as close to Jesus as he wanted to be. Then they asked him what the time was when I woke up. He told them the time. Dad had checked his watch when Mom told him—I would be all right. *Praise the Lord the time matched!* The anesthesiologist was in silent awe of the power of God. He then added, "From now on before I go into the operating room, I'm going to pray for the patient." How wonderful! He is probably retired now. But what healing miracles could occur in operating rooms, hospitals, clinics, and doctor's offices if medical professionals would silently pray for patients.

As far as the rest of my life's prognosis, I was more sickly with a lot of colds and ear and sinus infections; that was the only thing they had right. But my dad smoked a pipe for years, so without realizing at the time, secondary smoke might have caused some of that.

When I was a toddler, my parents took me to Lou's Health's Center in Youngwood Pennsylvania. Dr. Louis Bompioni was skilled in therapeutic massage. He's in heaven now, a grandson now runs the office, but he did not let his disability of blindness stop him from helping others. Despite complete blindness, he had a way of seeing things clearer than a sighted individual. Dr. Lou always had a big smile and enjoyed making balloon animals. With his help, I started talking at age three. Dad always joked that even though I was late in starting to talk, once I started, I never stopped.

I went to school by intercom. It was a telephone setup of sorts. If you wonder what the intercom looked like, there's an old movie called *Curse of Bigfoot* that actually showed one in use before the police went into the woods to get the monster. When it came time for college, I had been walking with two wooden canes for almost a decade. My legs were actually strong enough *to go to school.*

I also love how God has a sense of humor. Even though I was never on a school bus during first grade through twelfth grades, as an adult, I did ride a school bus. I guess the Lord wanted me to experience the camaraderie you can only get in that situation. At the time, my dad was still living and we were attending a Southern Baptist

Church. I wanted to be baptized, and the pastor and the deacons actually figured out how to safely immerse me. I was ecstatic and joined the church. Dad and I joined the choir. Each song lasted just a minute or two. Then the choir would sit a few minutes until the next song. Close to Christmas, the church would rent a school bus and go caroling to the elderly, ill, and a local nursing home. I loved that; there was a lot of walking and I had folding ice cleats for my canes. But you know the song "Leaning on the Everlasting Arms"? I relied on the Lord to keep me upright. He did! Also, I would rest in the bus between locations, and sometimes, it took a while, but what fun while riding in the bus since the singing and *fellowship continued.*

When my dad died unexpectedly over twenty years ago, Mom's and my world was turned upside down. We know that we will be reunited with Dad and other loved ones who have gone on before us someday. But starting with my dad's death, it seemed like Mom and I entered a season of Job that lasted for years. We had financial worries, I had appendicitis, and Mom had cataract surgery. Then in 2004, she had to have major stomach surgery for a life-threatening problem. *I don't know why we went through all that, but looking back on it now, it was like the poem "Footprints in the Sand." He carried us!*

In more recent years, I've had problems with leg weakness and back trouble. Some doctors have thought my cerebral might be worsening. They also say I have arthritis in my spine. My mother had a bad fall and has had some health issues since then. But praise the Lord she is zeroing in on a hundred. We now realize that even though over the years we have helped each other, we have reached the point where we need someone to help us with day-to-day physical tasks like cleaning, laundry, etc. After a lot of prayer, God has sent someone special into our lives to be our helper.

God has already shown me in the past what doctors say isn't the final say. I wonder if the stresses of these last years may have caused my problems. I'm standing on His promises and timing to heal Mom and me!

It would be great if we could always stay on the mountaintop throughout life until the Lord calls us home, but that is not realistic. When we all encounter those valleys in our lives and some valleys are deeper than others, that's when the devil tries his darnedest to discourage us. He knows if you have called on Jesus, your salvation is sealed by the Holy Spirit. But that does not stop him from trying to mess with our minds and emotions. The more he makes us think we are unable to do things or not able to do things as well as we used to—or if you're attempting something new and unsure, the better the devil likes it. If at times we get down fearing failure, he loves that. The devil hopes that if he can make us feel like screw-ups with the ordinary problems of life, we won't even attempt to do what God wants us to do and people will go unsaved. That's his plan. The devil wants to take as many people as he can with him and keep them *out of heaven. You have to ask God for His strength.* You cannot do it on your own and the devil will run!

> But be not far from me, O LORD: O my strength, haste thee to help me. (Ps. 22:19)

> Hast thou not known? Hast thou not heard, *that* the everlasting God, the Lord, the Creator of the ends of the earth, fainteth not, neither is weary? *There is* no searching of his understanding.
> He giveth power to the faint; and to *them that have* no might he increaseth strength.
> Even the youths shall faint and be weary, and the young men shall utterly fall:
> But they that wait upon the LORD shall renew *their* strength; they shall mount up with wings as eagles; they shall run, and not be weary; *and* they shall walk, and not faint. (This is a favorite verse of mine.) (Isa. 28–31; emphasis added)

> Submit yourselves therefore to God. Resist the devil, and he will flee from you. (James 4:7)

The interesting thing about this new season in my life at a time when I was beginning to think my ability to do *anything major* for

God was in my past—caroling, choir, helping in Bible school, church cantatas, and Dad and I were even in a living Christmas tree—God showed me otherwise. I almost believed the devil's lie that my usefulness to God was over or very limited. Praying for others is important, but I thought that was about all I could do. To my surprise, God had other plans.

Let's not forget Abraham, Moses, and Aaron were not spring chickens when the Lord called them into action. David was young when he faced Goliath. The Lord called Debra, Esther, and Ruth too. God calls whoever He wills—man or woman—at whatever age, young and old alike.

> So Abram departed, as the Lord had spoken unto him; and Lot went with him; and Abram *was* seventy and five years old when he departed out of Haran. (Gen. 12:4; emphasis added)

> And Moses *was* fourscore years old (eighty), and Aaron fourscore and three years old, when they spake unto Pharaoh. (Exod. 7:7; emphasis added)

One very important point when the Lord calls you to do something, *He* gives you what you need, to do what He wants you to accomplish. Whatever you do should glorify God since He gave you what you need. Take heed to what Jesus told His disciples. We can do *nothing without Him!*

> I am the true vine, and my Father is the husbandman.
> Every branch in me that beareth not fruit he taketh away: and every *branch* that beareth fruit, he purgeth it, that it may bring forth more fruit.
> Now ye are clean through the word which I have spoken unto you.

Abide in me, and I in you. As the branch cannot bear fruit of itself, except it abide in the vine; no more can ye, except ye abide in me.

I am the vine, ye *are* the branches: He that abideth in me, and I in him, the same bringeth forth much fruit: for without me you can do nothing.

If a man abide not in me, he is cast forth as a branch, and is withered; and men gather them, and cast *them* into the fire, and they are burned.

If ye abide in me, and my words abide in you, ye shall ask what ye will, and it shall be done unto you.

Herein is my Father glorified, that ye bear much fruit; so shall you be my disciples. (John 15:1–8; emphasis added)

When I was a teenager, I wrote a children's book, and a local publisher in my town was interested but wanted a rewrite to link the stories together. Before I could finish, I picked up the morning paper one day and was shocked to read the front page story. The publisher was filing for bankruptcy and closing. Luckily, no contract was signed, so I still had ownership of my work. Over the years, I submitted my book and other children's stories to other publishers. But no publisher was interested.

Then when I was in my twenties, the Lord gave me lyrics to a hymn. I had the words, but I cannot read music. Then we were invited to a Christian music concert at a local United Methodist Church. The singing group was the Vicksburg Quartet. It was a wonderful concert. When it was over, I got up the nerve to ask one of them if they knew anyone that might be interested in putting the music to my words. Later, an original member of the group came to our home with his keyboard. In short order, we had a song. A few weeks later, he called me to ask if they could put the song on their new cassette. To say I was on cloud nine was an understatement.

The Vicksburg Quartet had their own recording equipment. A member kept the equipment in his basement. Before they could record their new album, his basement was flooded. There was no insurance, and as a result, no album and *no song*.

After a few years, I was busy with the things of life. Also by this time, we were going to the Baptist Church I mentioned earlier and was enjoying church activities along with worshipping the Lord. I put the song and my writing in a filing cabinet by my bed. At the time, I just thought they were nice dreams, but I was in my early thirties when Dad died. As we entered that long season of Job, I completely forgot about them.

Then God started to show me our timing and His timing can be very different. It all started a week before Christmas a couple years ago. Mom and I were listening to a Christmas season sermon by Pastor David Jeremiah while making Christmas cookies. I wasn't thinking anything about lyrics or writing. My mind was centered on the sermon while my hands were busy rolling the cookie dough in balls. Out of the blue—and it had to be of God, not of me—nearly elbow deep in dough, came a phrase for a song. He did not speak it out loud but definitely sent the words in a thought.

Pastor Jeremiah's sermon was ending, and I wished the cookies were finished. I kept repeating the phrase so would not forget it before I would be able to write it down. I grabbed a lined tablet, but no additional words came that night. However, one week later, on Christmas Eve, I finished the Christmas hymn. Then over the next weeks and months, God led me to write four more songs. That brings my lyrics total now to six songs. I'm trying to find someone to take them to the next level. I pray they can bring people to the Lord. Every time I think I've found someone to meet with me and set these words to music, it falls through. If a Christian songwriter is interested in doing this, please contact Allie Lasher at Christian Faith Publishing so we can connect and put God's words to music. I look forward to hearing from someone.

I began to wonder about my dreams again. After all the years of what seemed to be failure, was God trying to tell me something! Was it just wishful thinking on my part or was He saying pick yourself up—

with my help—dust off the disappointment, get off your laurels, and get going? I did not have to wait long for the answer. One night, while Mom and I were sitting on the sofa watching television, a commercial came on for a Christian publishing company. The thought came, get the number, but no pen or paper was handy at the time. A few days later, I got the number. I checked them out with the better business bureau and submitted three sample stories to the company by fax and waited. After a nervous week, they said *yes! After all these years, dear Lord, thank you and let me never forget that you opened the door.*

The three stories were put together as a collection, *Meet Jebby, Jenny, and Laddie Boy*, for my first children's book, scheduled to be out by Christmas 2018. There is soon to be a second children's book. And if you are reading this, then the publishing company has approved my first adult book. Praise the Lord.

Years ago during the night, God gave me a special poem. He also wanted the words lined up a certain way. I quickly reached to turn my nightstand light on and grabbed a pen and small note pad. The thoughts came so fast I barely could keep up. The next day, I took my scribbled notes to my typewriter that had changeable type. I hope "The Cross" poem is an inspiration to you as it is to me.

Sarah Ankney

One last item I will mention before ending this testimony. After a lot of thinking about it, I chose the penname of Sarah Ankney. One day, I thought I better practice a signature. You might wonder why the *S* in Sarah is printed instead of written like the rest of the name. God showed me something special. In the Bible, it says to acknowledge God.

In all thy ways acknowledge him, and he shall direct thy paths.

Be not wise in thine own eyes: fear the LORD, and depart from evil.

It shall be health to the navel, and marrow to thy bones.

Honor the LORD with thy substance, and with the firstfruits of all thine increase:

So shall thy barns be filled with plenty, and thy presses shall burst out with new wine. (Prov. 3:6–10)

Commit thy works unto the LORD, and thy thoughts shall be established. (Prov. 16:3)

In plain English, put God first, don't think you know more than God, have reference for Him, and depart from evil and the evil things of this world. Honor the Lord—when you budget for your bills, give something to God before anything else. If you do this, it will help your health and God will provide for your needs.

The big *S* stands for several things:

First, *Son of God, Jesus* and putting him first in
 your life
Second, *Savior and Lord*
Third, *Salvation, that God and Jesus provide*
Fourth, *Spirit, the Holy Spirit; the comforter*

If you still have not accepted Jesus, please do so now or you may find yourself trapped by the little s's:

First: satan
Second: sin
Third: self; putting self first and never acknowl-
 edging God or others.

So please take self off the throne of your life meant for GOD. Admit your sin. Ask the *Son of God, Jesus,* to come into your life as *Savior and Lord.* Accept His *salvation* and the Holy *Spirit,* the comforter that seals us in the Lord. If you don't chose God, the alternative is Satan and the lake of fire.

So I hope my testimony encourages and inspires people to trust in God and His Son Jesus. Then accept Jesus as Savior and *prayerfully inquire what God wants you to do. Lastly, with His help, go do it!* I'm finding there is one thing harder than starting a testimony—it's finishing. So I feel led to let God's words finish the chapter and book with words from the last chapter of Hebrews.

> Now the God of peace, that brought again from the dead our Lord Jesus, that great shepherd of the sheep, through the blood of the everlasting covenant,
>
> Make you perfect in every good work to do his will, working in you that which is wellpleasing in his sight, through Jesus Christ; to whom *be* glory for ever and ever. Amen. (Heb. 13:20–21; emphasis added)

CHRIST

*S*on   of   God

*A*lpha and Omega

Jesus gave His *L*ife—in our place—to save us

And give us *V*ictory over sin and death

The Spirit of *A*doption—we can call him Abba

*T*rust the Lord

And obey

*I*nheritance of

Eternal life

*O*btain peace and

Joy

*N*ever cease to

Praise Him for

His blessings

W i t h o u t

N u m b e r !

How precious the gift of **SALVATION**.
Ask Him into your life *today*.

He said, "I will never leave thee nor forsake thee" (Heb. 13:5)

Appendix

Charities

There are many more charities than these; this is only a beginning to get you started. Also get involved local church outreach.

Village Missions
P O Box 197* 696 E Ellendale Ave
Dallas OR 97338-0197
800-617-9905

A nondenominational ministry that reaches out in many ways. Currently, it is involved in over 220 rural communities in the United States and Canada. It's working with people in rural areas to keep small churches open.

1. If a small community has their church closing, at the church's request, Village Missions can step in and help.
2. Provide pastors or missionaries.
3. People can donate to Village Missions or support pastors or missionaries in a certain church or rural area.
4. Contender's discipleship program—to train people to disciple in their local churches or training for working with village churches.

If you are a pastor who is retiring but still wants to continue preaching or if the Lord has called you to pastor in a small community, please call Village Missions or go to the website villagemissions. org.

Mercy Multiplied
P O Box 111060
Nashville TN 37222
615-831-6987
www.MercyMultiplied.com

A nonprofit Christian organization founded in 1983 with residential homes located in Monroe, LA; Nashville, TN; St Louis, MO; Lincoln, CA (A suburb of Sacramento); and international affiliates in the United Kingdom, Canada, and New Zealand.

1. Dedicated to helping young women ages thirteen to twenty-eight break free from life-controlling behaviors and situations, including eating disorders, self-harm, drug and alcohol addictions, unplanned pregnancy, depression, sexual abuse, and sex trafficking, through its free of charge residential program.
2. Mercy Multiplied's outreach activities are designed to educate leaders, equip individuals, and empower churches. Our programs and resources are based on the same biblically based, life-transforming principles used by Mercy homes for over thirty years in helping troubled young women find lasting freedom and live an empowered Christian life.
3. MPower Workshops can help you understand more about life-controlling issues, steps to helping and supporting others, and how to stay healthy and whole in the process.

Crossing Paths Ministries
670 Dutch Lane
Hermitage PA 16148
724-981-7777
don@crossingpaths.org

A television ministry with an emphasis on the saving grace of Jesus Christ. Guests also give their personal testimonies of what Christ has done for them.

1. Provides free pocket Bibles for anyone that requests one.
2. Often highlights other ministries on their program. The ministry can also help people connect to various ministries like food banks, Christian-based drug and alcohol programs, etc.

Joni and Friends
P O Box 3333
Agoura Hills CA 91372-3333
Phone 818-707-5664
Product Orders 800-736-4177
Fax 818-707-2391
Joniandfriends.org

A ministry created to help people with disabilities and their families. Also, it promotes awareness of disability issues with churches and other groups. Emphasis on the sanctity of life.

1. Radio and television program.
2. Retreats for disabled and families both in the United States and other countries.
3. Giving wheelchairs in other countries
4. Christian Institute on Disability: courses to educate ministers and churches how to minister to the disabled and internships for leadership in disability ministry. Also brings

biblical perspective on public policy on hotly debated disability related issues like stem cell research.

5. You can give donations for people in the internships or provide housing for students in internships.

6. If you are interested in the services provided or want to volunteer, just go to the website and plug in your zip code.

7. Website has books about disability, aids for churches, etc. Also sells cards and planners. You can also donate.

Wallbuilders.com
Founder David Barton

1. Founded to get the word out about America's forgotten history with emphasis on our moral and Christian heritage.

2. Please check out the website to see how you can help.

References

For portion of chapter 12 as related to humanized mice and use of aborted baby body parts.

Russell, Donna. "FDA Buys Baby Body Parts from Company Investigated for Selling Human Tissue for Profit." CBN News, August 10, 2018. www1.cbn.com/cbnnews/us/2018/august/fda-buys-baby-body-parts-from-company-investigated-for-selling-human-tissue-for-profit

Warren, Steve. "85 Members of Congress Denounce FDA Contract with Company Supplying Tissue from Aborted Babies." CBN News, September 17, 2018. https://www1.cbn.com/cbnnews/politics/2018/september/members-of-congress-denounce-fda-contract-with-company-supplying-tissue-from-aborted-babies

Jones, Emily. "Trump Admin Says NIH Will No Longer Conduct Research Using Aborted Baby Body Parts." CBN News, June 06, 2019. https://www1.cbn.com/cbnnews/us/2019/june/trump-admin-says-nih-will-no-longer-conduct-research-using-aborted-baby-body-parts

CBN News. "Biden Admin Allows 'A Marketplace for Aborted Baby Body Parts' Using Taxpayer Money." CBN News, April 19, 2021. https://www1.cbn.com/cbnnews/politics/2021/april/a-marketplace-for-aborted-baby-body-parts-biden-admin-to-allow-fetal-tissue-research-using-taxpayer-money

About the Author

Sarah Ankney is a physically challenged woman who enjoys painting and writing, especially children's books. She hopes someday to team up with someone with music knowledge to turn lyrics into songs. She also loves the Lord and the Pennsylvania mountains.

Printed in the USA
CPSIA information can be obtained
at www.ICGtesting.com
CBHW020119130824
12995CB00001B/8

9 781639 035540